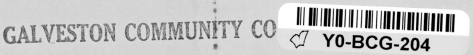

THREE SIDES
TO
THE RIVER

THREE SIDES
TO
THE RIVER

by
ESTELLE CARRUTH

The Naylor Company
Book Publishers of the Southwest
San Antonio, Texas

DEDICATED

to

Margarethe Meyer Anderson

FOREWORD

And Ruth said, Intreat me not to leave thee, or to return from following after thee: for whither thou goest, I will go; and where thou lodgest, I will lodge: thy people shall be my people and thy God my God.
Where thou diest, will I die, and there will I be buried; the Lord do so to me, and more also, if ought but death part thee and me.

THE BOOK OF RUTH
Chapter I, verses 16 and 17

CONTENTS

ONE

YOUR
telephone is an innocent-looking instrument, lying there, completely relaxed in its little cradle. Silent, taking up little space, no time, and making no demands, you can completely ignore it. You can until it takes your life in its cradle and starts molding and twisting and turning and shaping things.

You give little thought to the telephone until years later. Then you realize it all started with the telephone call. It seems even more strange when you realize you did not ever know how the call came about, from someone you did not know, from a place of which you had never heard. With no warning, the telephone started the whole chain of events that changed the courses of so many lives.

A voice I had never heard, from a place I was not then sure how to pronounce, said, "This is Miss James of the Social Welfare Board in Chaparral. The Mexican classroom needs an English teacher. If you would like to teach English to Mexicans, we will pay a hundred and thirty a month."

I knew why I went. That big salary! I had never had a bank account. I had never had the things I needed, to say nothing of the many things I merely wanted. I had been with Mexicans, within a regular classroom as a part of my college work. I had never seen an all-Mexican classroom. I thought I would really enjoy that. It was a challenge to see what I might be able to learn from this new experience. Since the death of my only

1

living relative, a distant aunt, I was eager to leave Musgrove — to go away, anywhere, just to get away from Musgrove. I soon forgot about the salary since it did not get me any of the things I merely wanted; with the hotel and food bills to pay, it was originally the reason I went. That big salary!

The call came about four o'clock in the afternoon, and it was six by the time I had all my earthly possessions in the almost-new Ford. The almost-new Ford was the reason I had so very few possessions; I was still making payments.

I remember that it was a dark, pleasantly cool, September night, with big stars overhead that did almost nothing to the highway, nothing at all to the ground. It was bright above and black on the ground. I remember that I felt the wind on my face and that I would toss my head at the way the wind blew the page-boy hair across my face. I kept throwing my head around and spitting out the strands. That was before the pony tail. In 1940 you let it blow and spit it out.

I remember the thrill and the almost-can't-wait excitement of going to a new job — any job. I had planned to go to college in September on borrowed money again, and I was getting cold feet at the prospect. The offer of the job was a godsend in more ways than one. I remember the broad, level, almost-never-a-turn Texas highway with just me on it. I drove faster and faster across the far reaches of the vacant space with the wind in my face and a song in my heart.

It was not a lovely ride. I was in too much of a hurry to find the new life. It was a happy aloneness. The voice from my radio was singing, "Tumbling Tumbleweed," as the tumbleweeds rolled unevenly, skipping across the broad highway in front of the Ford. The wind gave up just a little and the weeds jammed in front of the car in silent bravery and defiance. A coyote wailed in the distance — a lonesome eerie sound, as the jack rabbits ran across the road. The moon shed a little light. Mesquite and cactus became more distinct. This — this was my heritage, this background of space and nothingness, but always something of desert splendor to one born to it. I guess I love it. I did not know it then. Years later, the outlines of the prairie night — that night — stand out like black etchings. In all this aloneness, I had no feeling of being alone.

2

I was twenty when I went to Chaparral. That was my first teaching job and I was already looking forward to many years of the excitement of teaching school. The future constituted the hopes and the plans and all the dreams I ever had — the dreams of the young, the dreams of the rosy land of promise.

Driving into Chaparral had been like driving into a tunnel — buildings on both sides. That building on the right must be the high school. That would be the American High School, since there was no other one here. There was no light there except the dim light that proclaimed a building as the "Hotel Vidaurri. American Cuisine. American Guests. Vacancy."

The hotel was a square, white, red-tiled top, stucco, made to look like adobe; remotely, that is, it looked like adobe. It had a second story over only about a third of it. This gave it a very peculiar shape, as if some recluse had built a penthouse on one end of the top.

Ophelia met me at the door. Ophelia overshadowed the lobby, its furnishings, the night clerk, and the very night. Her straight shining, brown hair was cut like mine, slightly turned up at the ends. It was heavy and springing like the ads say the shampoo will make your hair spring. Olive skin, sort of coffee with heavy cream, and smooth looking — smooth as velvet — made me want to touch it to see if it really felt like velvet. Her green — or were they grey — eyes made a strange and effective contrast with her hair.

I was staring at her and thinking that no girl who looked like that should have to work for her living. She smiled a sweet, welcoming smile and said, "I'm Ophelia Gorman. The rest of the working girls are out — out on the town — or just out. After all, it is Friday night, and even though we all have to work Saturdays — all except you — Friday night is a special night. It is on par with Saturday night for date night, and I never thought to wonder why. It just is."

And to the hotel clerk she said, "Cava, this is Miss Camish. Mr. Smith said she was to have the single room next to mine. Isn't that wonderful?"

"Yes'm, it sho' is," replied Cava, though I was not sure what was wonderful. With barely a glance in my general direction, Cava said, "I'll carry that bag, Miss Gorman. Any other suitcases? No? Well — Well, I declare."

We climbed the short flight of threadbare stairs. (I learned later where the holes were so that I could miss them all in the dark.) Ophelia was leading the way with the aid of Cava's flashlight, which did not have a very powerful bulb — a very dim sort of guide. I can see her now, as I walked along behind her how trim and smart she was and always how she held her head so high as if she owned everything she touched. She tossed her luxuriant hair, looked back at me, and said, as if it were a lovely joke, "Watch the holes in the carpet, Jennie. Be careful."

Out of the dimness Cava said, "I know what Mr. Smith say. He tell me before he and she go to the show. I know where the guests live, Miss Gorman." Sulky, as though he had just thought to say it.

Ophelia said, "I'm just thoughtless Cava. You take such good care of all of us. I know you know all about this hotel."

He was mollified. "Yes'm."

You go up this short flight of steps, turn left, walk past two doors, and open your own door where there is no carpet to stub your foot on. There is a small, single bed, white enamel, old-fashioned, not antique, lumpy-looking, and covered with a white — once white — counterpane. You see an old rocker, not an antique. One table doubles as a desk, a catchall, and anything else it may eventually be needed for. One dresser, high, old, with knobs on the drawers mostly missing, and you discover later, after almost everybody you meet has worked on them, that the drawers don't shut when they are open or open when they are shut; so you learn to leave them open as the others learned long ago. The mirror does queer contortions to your face, like the kind you used to see at the carnival. There is one bare bulb, with few watts, dangling from the center of the ceiling. The fixtures in the bathroom are white. Well, almost. They once were white, but they are a little rusty and corroded in spots where the water drips — always and forever, the water drips. You hang up your best dress, push your bag under the bed, and ask Ophelia, "Where on earth did Cava get that name? He isn't Mexican."

"No, he's mostly Negro, but the features are Indian. He's, nobody knows how old. All bent over with rheumatism like that, and the white hair, and the Indian features of the face,

4

with almost no wrinkles. Nobody knows who he is or where he came from."

"The name is Mexican, isn't it?" I asked.

She laughed. "No, his name is George Washington Carver Jones. He wants to be called Carver; but when he says it, it comes out Cava, so Cava he is."

I went to sleep on the lumpy mattress, enfolded in a million dreams of all the wonderful things that may happen this year, this first year of a long teaching career. I could hardly wait until morning. I had not a care in the world, and I slept the sleep of youth — the youth that has no cares. Suddenly, it was morning.

Ophelia came out of the adjoining bathroom in flats and a tweed skirt and plaid shirt, looking more feminine than most girls do in heels and lace and ruffles.

"I'm going over to the church study," she said. "Brother Way is such a fine man, and I enjoy working with him; I do as much of the typing as I have time and help with teaching a Sunday school class though I'm afraid I don't do very well with that. That's your field."

Oh, no, not mine. I would be scared silly. But, yes, I would go over with her. I met the preacher, who was small, fair, and quite ordinary-looking. He had a good voice. I could see he would be influential from his pulpit. After I met the preacher, I set out at nine o'clock on Saturday morning to see this new and exciting land — this foreign land — this magic land.

I walked the length of the town which was built around a square. That took ten minutes. Then, I started over. The square was a maze of color: zinnias of every hue. Narrow paths ran among the flowers and in the center was a badly done statue of George Washington. Evergreens had been planted at odd spots with no view to planning, as if they just grew wild. Rustic benches set around the trees and around the statue did not look inviting; the park was not a thing of beauty.

I got two blocks from the Vidaurri to the town's one cafe. It was on the bottom floor of a long, narrow, unpainted wood building. It was rather large, since it had all the business in town, that is, the eating business. Now, going to eat and going out to eat were two different things. "Let's go eat" meant go

5

to Lee's. "Let's go to dinner" meant Holtville. Lee's had one wall solid with a food bar and stools. The rest of the space was taken up with square tables that seated four. When a larger party came in, they just pushed the tables together and arranged space for their own party. Here, on a stool, I ordered a coke which I did not drink.

I heard Lee say, "We don't serve Meskins in here. Now, get out! Go on back to your own town. You got a town of your own; go eat there."

I choked on my drink. He — the Mexican — walked slowly out, very straight, and with all the dignity his race can muster, and that is a great deal. All eyes followed his retreating back as if he were a diamondback rattler they hoped would not turn on them.

Then Lee, the manager of the cafe, said in her masculine voice, "That one went to some college. That one, he don't belong here in the first place. College. That ruins them ever' time."

Giggles and loud jokes and all of this nine miles from the river that separates the United States and Mexico, in a small town with about a third of the people Mexican.

I looked at this man; I watched him leave, and my throat ached, and I had a knot in my chest. This man was just like anybody, anybody you might meet anywhere. What had he done? I felt a deep fear, a nameless fear, and a fury unfounded. That is, I did not know what it was founded on. I had just never seen a decent human being so snubbed. What could he have done?

I went out on the street. He was standing on the street corner looking into space with a sort of glazed stare. He was taller than most Mexicans, but with the same black hair, black eyes and bronze skin. He was not as handsome as many of them. He was thinner and cleaner and neater. He looked completely crushed, as if he did not know what to do next. His face did; but he was standing very straight, tall, and still.

I walked up beside him and touched his arm to get his attention. I did not know what I was going to do, but I somehow wanted to apologize for the insult. He jumped as though

6

I had dealt him a hard, surprise blow. His slightly oriental eyes became bare slits.

"Don't come near me. Don't be seen talking to a Mexican. You are new here, or you'd know that. Keep walking. Go on."

"But, I just wanted to say . . . "

"Don't say anything to me, now or ever. Never. Go on. Go away."

I did not move, so he did. He walked off, very fast, toward Little Mexico.

The rest of Saturday I had to myself. The day had suddenly become too long, stretching way out in front of me and lonely — lonely. This man had asked for a ham sandwich to take out, and he was just like anybody you might know. He was certainly somebody I would like to know! I did not understand it.

"You betta git yo' nap on Sat'dys an' Sund'ys Ma'am. Won't be no time next week. School starts up agin. They all gits they see-esta aroun' heah, and times is too short in the work week."

Cava's advice was well-meant, and I realized I was probably the only woman in town awake. I couldn't go to sleep, but I got my siesta, prone, watching the hill and wondering, after the display of attitude I had just seen, what my status as the English teacher would be. What had I gotten myself into? This was a sort of far-off wondering. My bitterness was directed at them — not being sure who or what *they* were. Who could cut this boy so deeply for no reason, or was there a reason I did not know about?

Saturday night the town came to life. The ranchers and their wives came in from the ranches ten to a hundred miles away. They came in Cadillacs, Buicks, pickup trucks and Fords. They wore big Stetson hats, tailor-made whipcord pants and jackets, bright scarves and special order Justin boots — men and women. I never did figure out who wore tighter pants, the women or the men. They gossiped and drank coffee and walked up and down the street, drank coffee in the lobby; and when they got tired or sleep, or wanted a stronger drink, they went to their rooms. They were using rooms they reserved weekend after weekend. They reserved them by being there every weekend, or because past generations of their families had been there

7

every weekend. Or, some of the rooms might have been paid for by somebody they beat in a poker game, or somebody to whom they had lost in a poker game last Saturday night, or this Saturday night if they stayed up long enough or if the men played poker long enough. It was a weekend ritual. They were getting louder and louder and I was wondering what to do with myself when Ophelia came in.

She came in bubbling all over, like a hidden spring with an unknown source. "I have a friend here, down in the lobby. Just a friend. You must meet him, but first I have to open up the shop for a few hours. Friday nights and Saturday nights are when I do my best business. The men spend money like mad; they put it on the women's backs. I have the only exclusive shop in town, and they buy me out every Friday and and Saturday night. The rest of the week, well, I just stay open."

"You own a dress shop?"

"Oh, no. I just manage it. Mr. Falop owns it. He's a nice boss; leaves me alone and lets me work on commission. I have the best looking things in the country, and I want you to see it."

Ophelia's shop was two blocks from the Vidaurri in the opposite direction from Lee's Cafe. You would think she had on a dollar-day special to break all records. When she opened the shop at seven in the evening every rancher within a hundred-mile radius was there with his wife, to literally buy Ophelia out. The women would glance at a garment or feel of the material, or say she liked that, and he would ask how much as he reached for a roll of bills. Ophelia could have made a living working only from seven to ten on Friday and Saturday evenings. She almost did. They stood in line and bought everything they saw. I believe they would have bought anything, anything at all their women took a fancy to. I stared, open-mouthed and hungry. I had never seen so much money in my life. I had never seen such good-looking clothes, and I had never owned anything that looked like even one dress in Ophelia's shop. If a redhead wanted a color and style that screamed at her hair, her husband said, "You look awful sweet in that, Hon. Give her that, Ophelia. You got anything else real pretty for her?"

8

"Heard about that Mexican feller goin' in Lee's today. Don't that beat all? Give 'em a inch, they'll take a mile. Wasn't for the ranchers, they wouldn't even make a living. It does beat all."

The lovely clothes lost interest for me almost as I became interested. The Mexicans worked on the cattle ranches. They worked long and hard and were not over-paid. If they had not made a living here, they would have gone some other place. If they had not done the work, the ranchers might have had to do more — and they thought they were giving something away.

I slipped out, planning to go to bed. I got undressed and was in bed trying to figure the Mexican situation when Ophelia came in. I dressed and went downstairs to meet Bob. Bob was a big businessman. He dressed like one, talked like one, acted like one, and was from an oil company in Oklahoma. I do not know as a fact that Bob was a big businessman. I assumed all these things because he was not like men I had met or seen. Though I never knew how big his desk was or how many cubic feet had been allotted to him for the desk, an oil man from Oklahoma was big business.

He was also big and masculine and looked at Ophelia as if he adored her. She fluttered her eyes and wriggled when she walked and exuded femininity all over. I did not know this night that this was not an act, but was Ophelia at any time. It did not look exactly like friendship to me, but then my experience had been limited.

They showed me my first taste of night life in Chaparral. The ranchers' wives had changed to dresses now. The women were wearing elaborate and revealing formals.

"Jennie, her dress alone, the cost of it, would see you well-dressed for a year. I know. I sold it to her."

"You dress like they do?" was a request for information from me, I suppose, or curiosity.

"No," Ophelia said. "I get mine wholesale, or I could never do as well as I do. I've always been interested in style and what constitutes style, and I study it. I get the most I can for my money, to look right for me. Some of my clothes don't cost as much as they appear to."

She was wearing a gold taffeta dress with shoes dyed to

9

match. The dress gave her hair a gold sheen and even her eyes had gold flecks in them. That is, the gold showed. I noticed for the first time that she had the smallest feet I had ever seen on an adult — small and narrow and the highest heels in which she could not only walk, but dance. She wore no jewelry.

By ten o'clock, when Ophelia closed the shop, the ranchers' wives had on their jewelry. I had to stare at the size and the number of diamonds and think they could not be real — they did not make them that big.

"There are more millionaires here than in any other place this size in America," Cava told me.

"Is that so?"

"It may or may not be so, Jennie," Ophelia said. "I've always heard that, and I have also heard it about other ranch towns and about oil towns. I think they all like to claim this if they are a moneyed town."

The dance hall was the large top floor of the cafe. Lee was doing a thriving business below, and the floor above was crowded. It was not dance atmosphere. It was carnival atmosphere, even to the dance barker. It was easy to see that these people had little respect for money. They were trying too hard to get rid of it. Nobody wanted anybody else to pay for anything.

"Here, I'll get that," a man would say and pull out a wad of big bills from his shirt pocket, or his hip pocket. I never knew how he could get the money in the hip pocket with the pants hugging him so tightly, but there they carried some of it. Money was something with which to play poker and have fun. There was so much of it, you could almost feel it floating around in the air. It made you feel much like a pauper. I always wondered what they did with the fives and the tens; nobody ever paid for anything with less than a twenty-dollar bill, and often it was a fifty or a hundred. Lee was new, but she was prepared for making change. She was a heavy-set redhead and was coining tips like the mint. I knew she was new because everybody told me. All they wanted to know was, "Is she married?"

The dance floor was so crowded you could not move, but you had to get out there. Everybody did. You didn't need a date.

10

Cowboys were six deep all around the wall. One of them told me, "This is no dance floor. This is Lee's Ballroom."

Bob and Ophelia looked like a couple out of a story book. He was blond and rugged. His nose was too long, his face sort of square, and his eyes said nothing. Put together, he came out handsome, perhaps because he was every woman's dream of the masculine. They danced like a dream, slow and dreamy and easily.

Perry worked for Bob. He was less of a big shot, less huge physically and seemed to be filled with less of the feeling of his own importance. He was dark, about my height and nice to dance with.

I met the same people that night, over and over, that I would be introduced to over and over in the future until finally everybody would know me and think they knew more about me than I knew about myself. After a while they all began to look alike; they dressed and acted so much alike. They danced alike. It was a matter of who could stomp the loudest, move the fastest, and bump into each other the hardest.

I met Mr. and Mrs. Smith that night. He was a tall, dignified-looking man around seventy. She looked forty, but she may have been older. Her hair had been dyed so many times I never knew its true color. We stopped downstairs in the cafe for coffee, and the new redhead was saying, "That's one reason I wanted to come here. The owner said they would not put up with the Meskins actin' like white people. You hear about the Meskin boy trying to eat in here?"

A three-piece Mexican orchestra was playing the dance upstairs!

"He didn't try to eat here. He just ordered a ham sandwich to take out."

My words were met with the silence of death, but not the respect. Hostile, unbelieving looks were directed at me. Nobody said a word until Perry, in embarrassment, said, "Drink your coffee and let's go."

Just out of the light and on the edge of the sidewalk was a Mexican mother and two little girls. In their shy, sweet, tentative way they each said softly, one at a time as though they wanted only me to hear, "Hallo, teasher."

11

Their warm, soft smiles had a tentative look as though they had barely dared to do this. I warmed all over. These were to be my people, my children and my mothers. When I spoke as warmly, Perry's hand tightened on my arm as though he must protect me from criminal attack and urged me on. They followed us at a distance, slowly, always staying just in the dark.

I looked back and Bob and Ophelia and the Smiths were just behind us, and all of them looked to be in a state of shock, all except Ophelia, that is, who showed nothing, nothing at all but sweetness and light as though she had not seen. We walked silently to the hotel and went to the Smith's apartment.

Bert, the hotel manager, and his wife, Lou, had an apartment on the ground floor. They stayed in it most of the time they were in town. It was ornate to the point of very poor taste and over-stuffed with furniture and whatnots to the point of being ridiculous. It was a grand place for coffee, for telling your troubles, or listening to the marvelous stories of all the places they had been. At first it was.

The minute you walked into their apartment, you felt as if you had known them forever. His "Just call me Bert" and Lou's "I'm Lou" took no get-acquainted period. Lou was the one who set this pace with her warm generosity. He was quiet, and I could not imagine his dignity bending one iota. They were an odd combination. How did they ever get together? She was a dark, silent, little-young thing; whatever her age, she was eternally young.

They — all of them — seemed to have no use for the Mexicans, and even Ophelia had been noncommittal. To whom could I talk? I felt that Ophelia should have been the one; but, thus far, she had kept clear of any conversation having to do with the Mexicans. I thought I would wait until we were in our rooms, and then I would try to talk with her.

"Why won't Lee serve Mexicans in the cafe?" My words surprised me as much as anyone else. They just came out. There was no indication that I was going to broach the subject, and I felt the same amazement but not the shock. What had been the noisiest group I had ever heard a few minutes earlier was now the quietest. Frozen, unbelieving, shocked expressions were all aimed directly at me. I felt completely nude, as if my clothes had all suddenly fallen at my feet. The quiet held for a few seconds which seemed endless. Lee, the redhead from the cafe walked in and as I turned I faced her. She made a feeble attempt to smile, took two steps toward me, stopped, released the smile, looked around slowly at each person, saw no help anywhere, and started over. She pulled at the smile again and took two more steps which put her in front of me. Desperately, she grabbed for a sweet voice she did not own. I remember thinking how easy it would be for me to just step out the window, get into the Ford and start driving back to Musgrove.

She said, "Jennie, nobody in Chaparral serves Mexicans in any of the stores, or at the hotel, or anywhere. They have their own town."

Bob said, "I'd think you would know that."

"How would I know it?" I asked.

Lou said, "Anybody would know that."

Bert said, "Yes, it would seem so, my dear."

"I still don't see how I would know it," I insisted.

Lee said, "Honey, they don't need to come to Chaparral at all. They can get anything *they* need in Little Mexico."

"How long have you been here?" I asked.

"That has nothing to do with it," she said. "I know Mexicans. They lie and cheat, and they're filthy. I've lived around them all my life."

I noticed that Lee's neck looked dirty, and I almost asked her why she did not take a bath.

Perry said, "Why don't you lay off? Give her a little time. She doesn't know what she's talking about."

Bert rediscovered that he was the host. "That's it," he said. "How about another round of coffee, Mama?"

Mama got real busy, real fast, and most of her guests followed her into the little kitchenette, ostensibly to help her pour coffee into Haviland china cups. I hesitated precariously, half in and half out of the low window, wanting an answer to my question — my all-pervading question. There just wasn't anything else. Combined forces came back into the room with Lee still the spokesman.

"Now, Honey. You just relax and drink your coffee and tell me what you're talking about. Lou, fix me another salty dog, Baby."

13

Lee was not quite sober. She usually was the spokesman because usually she was not quite sober.

They took it, tensely and rigidly, until I got to the place where I had walked up to the Mexican fellow on the street corner. They just could not believe that.

Bob said, "No. You didn't really?"

Bert said, "Now, did you do that, Jennie?"

Lou looked at me sort of quizzically.

I said, "I'm telling you I did. That's just how it happened."

Lee said, "Get her, Perry," as if I could get away.

We went back to the ballroom above Lee's. I did not know why. It was time for the dance to be over.

I had begun to think that the only friend I had in all of Chaparral was Perry; or in the Vidaurri where paces were set, social mores were long-established and the issues of the town decided. I did not belong here, or I could not get in until I discovered why. I had to understand. If this Mexican had committed a crime, he should be punished, not insulted. Then I knew he could not be at fault. Why? I do not know.

"Perry, what did I do wrong? And also . . . "

"You didn't do anything wrong, Hon. We're going by the orchestra now, Hon. This way. Dance almost over."

We squirmed our way to the area on which the orchestra stood. The orchestra was composed of a guitar, a bass fiddle, and a violin. They were playing, and the one with the guitar was singing "Deep in the Heart of Texas" with a Mexican accent. We were doing well. We ran head-on into another couple who did not even look up. Perry had not realized the accepted practice of stomping here. He was from Tulsa. I did not realize it; I realized so few things. I rapidly decided I knew almost nothing about almost everything.

"Will you tell me why they all freeze and glare when I talk about that Mexican? I want to know, please."

"Listen, Hon." And then he stopped. He was trying to go on. He either did not know how to tell me or how much to tell me. "Listen, now. You're a nice kid and I like you. I want to see you again. We're having a good time, and let's not spoil it by talking about the Mexicans. They are not worth it. Don't worry about it any more. Just try to follow me, and

14

we'll try to keep in 'stomp' with these others. How they dance in cowboy boots I'll never know."

I gave up and shut up — but temporarily.

"Very well. I'm going to stay here. I'm having fun, and this is going to be a wonderful year, and I'll find out later. I'll learn if I have to stay here the rest of my life." They were playing "Be Honest With Me," and I wondered why nobody would.

Perry walked me back to the hotel lobby where Cava was, between drinks, telling a bewildered couple, "No'me, you ain't got no reservations 'cause this is Sat-dy nite, and I don't care what it says on the register; it's still Sat'dy nite."

Perry turned, walked me back to the dance floor at Lee's; and, as we walked on, the three-man orchestra struck up "Rancho Grande," and a long, slim cowboy grabbed me. He did not ask permission; he did not look my way. He did not smile. He did not tag me. He grabbed me, and I looked back at Perry expecting to be rescued.

"Go ahead, Hon," he said.

The cowboy walked on my feet and said, "What are you doing with that dumb oil boy? You look like a real nice sort of gal."

I walked on his feet and said, "Well, I think I am, and I don't think it is any of your business." That will stop him, I thought. Oh, yes? It opened him up. He laughed as though I had said something clever, then he very tolerantly explained.

"You're new here. Just 'cause you teach Mexicans don't make no difference. All the American teachers are married, but no oil boy gonna get the one single teacher in Little Mexico. One of 'em got the Mexican teacher a few years ago. We swore that'd never happen again. Now, Jennie, that's your name isn't it? Teaching Mexicans don't make you no different to no other teacher. Just 'cause you're the only one teaches Meskins, you just get that out of your head. You don't have to put up with no oil boy. No Sir-ee. Don't make no difference. Them oil tycoons got nothin' to offer. Don't you want a home? How you know he's not married? I been tellin' Ophelia this for two years and I intend to keep on till she listens to me. She will sometime."

The dance was over, and I had not said a word since the

very beginning. Bert grabbed me. One dance and I knew they always grab you. You could come to Lee's Ballroom every Saturday night until you were a very old woman, and still they'd grab you.

"Don't pay any attention to the oil boys, Jennie. Don't pay any attention to the ranchers. Pay close attention to the man, Jennie. That's all that really matters. Cowboys don't like anybody not cattle ranch coming in here. Don't like us, never did. Just take us as a necessity. I can spot a married man the minute I see one. Been in this business forty years. If one comes in that door, I'll tell you if he's married. I'll know. Go with anybody you want to Jennie — cowboy, oil man, rancher. It makes no difference," Bert explained.

He had said the most sensible things I had heard but he had not said I could go with a Mexican.

Perry was standing on the side line with the stags, several dozen pairs of boots near the table, watching the poker game. The women stood just behind the flimsy wood rail but they never crossed it. There were also two other fellows with shoes on.

"Why did you let that stupid cowboy dance with me?"

"That's the only thing I could do, Hon. There are only three of us here tonight. Bob and me and that fellow in there talking to Cava. I don't know him, but he's an oil boy. There he comes now. Count the boots, Hon. Want to get me killed? Wait. Some night we will outnumber them."

We went out to the square. Something had happened to the little square since morning. The zinnias were bright, and the moonlight gave them a fresh-washed look and sort of covered them with a silver glow. The trees were dark and glowing and somehow mysterious. The moon was sliding down the back of the church, just behind a purple-at-night hill in the distance. We sat on the bench in the zinnia bed by a tree, and I put my head on Perry's shoulder. I wanted to sob my heart out for all the things that had happened in the past twenty-four hours.

TWO

"NEVER in a million years will I understand this place."

"Yes you will, Jennie. Just listen more and talk less. That's the way Ophelia plays it and everybody likes her, Mexicans and whites. Take your time. These little border towns are not like other towns. They take a while to know. Nobody can tell you how to feel, Jennie. Some things you will have to make your own mind up about. You'll have to decide how you feel about a lot of things."

He might not tell me how to feel, but he had told me how he felt when he referred to Anglos as whites.

"No, Jennie. I won't explain anything to you. If I did, I'd be telling you how to feel about things no matter how hard I tried not to. I'd be telling you what to think and too much of that goes on around here."

I wondered if he knew he had already told me, and it only made me still want to talk to somebody who would explain things to me.

"What's that peculiar light in the hills there?"

"That's morning, Hon, and you'd better get to bed if we're going to have breakfast together."

We went back to the ballroom. It was empty — almost. The poker game was going strong. It was all right to watch but not to giggle or burp or make a sound.

"I'll cover ye."

17

"I'll raise ye one." And the man nonchalantly threw down a thousand-dollar bill as if it were a piece of dirty paper.

It was a quiet and orderly and calm poker game — a very serious business. Nobody had been drinking, or else they were all so drunk it did not show. They seemed to know exactly what they were doing. Stragglers were still watching; they'd wander up and down the long flight of narrow, wood steps that led down to the cafe, which was closed, but open for coffee. You got your own coffee and left the money on the table where Lee had set up the big coffee urn.

"They'll take him before the night is over. Crazy nut. Ought to have enough sense to stay away from them."

"Well, tell him." I said to Perry.

"You can't do that," he said. "He'll know tomorrow when he wakes up broke. Tomorrow Bob and I will see if he needs any money and go pay his hotel bill before he gets down. I learned that here. That's the way the oil boys do it."

"Who is he?"

"Never saw him in my life. He's in an oil company car."

"You want in, feller?"

That was Hank. The cowboy who had told me, between our stepping on each other's feet, about oil boys.

"No, thanks, feller, but thank you just the same."

This Hank gave me a withering look, slapped down another one, and then somebody said, "Make it two," and I said, "I'm sleepy."

Down the narrow, steep wood stairs, the two blocks to the Vidaurri, up the short flight of stairs with the worn carpet to the corner of the partial top floor where the working girls lived, and I asked, "You wanta come in?"

"No," he said. "Just give me a ring when you wake up, and I'll meet you in the lobby and take you to breakfast."

Lee came in about four o'clock in the morning. She made enough noise to wake everybody in the hotel, but I seemed to be the only one awake. Lee lived just two doors and across the hall from me. She undressed and prepared for bed with much singing, splashing of water, and banging into things.

Then, from farther down the hall I heard, "Listen you, Fred.

18

Why did you drink so much? Come on to bed. Now, get to bed."

I felt ordinary and tawdry and sleepy — and guilty, I suppose. Guilty for the treatment of a man whose name I did not know, but whose name I intended to find out. When I awakened, the sun was pouring in, a brilliant glare — blinding.

"I've been waiting for you to wake up," Ophelia said.

She had on pink today. Pink cotton, expensive-looking and with the ever-present tiny, high-heeled shoes, a pink sweater and the little purse to match. I put on my red dress which was, after all, my Sunday dress, and we went down to the lobby.

Cava said, "Miss Ophelia. I can jes' tell you got a good night's sleep. You look all rested and pretty. You get any sleep, Miss Jennie?"

I don't know what time Ophelia came in, or where she had been most of the night.

"Heah is a note for you from yo' gentemum frens. It say they got to go back to Oklahoma. The big boss he call and you and Miss Jennie asleep. They say they be back when they can git back. Heah the note."

There was no point in reading it, but Ophelia extended her hand as though he were offering her a precious gift.

"Thank you, Cava," she said sweetly.

We sat on the veranda in the old-fashioned rockers, sat peacefully and looked at the hill in front of us. So, it wasn't the high school as I had thought. She said the oil boys never knew when they would be called and to think nothing about it. She gave me time to mention Bob and Perry, and when she knew I was not going to, she did.

"How did you like Perry?" she asked.

"He's nice."

After further pauses she said, "I think I'm in love with Bob."

"You *think* you're in love? I thought you'd know."

"I guess I do."

Hank sauntered by, slowed his easy pace, gave Ophelia an adoring look, stuck his thumbs in the top of his pants, sauntered off and slowly slid under the wheel of his Cadillac.

"Now, if you want money and plenty of it, there's one for you. If you want anything else, that's not it."

She laughed long when I told her about our dance and his advising me about the oil boys last night.

Back in her room we put on slacks and shirts and prepared to listen to records.

"Who lives in that next room?" I asked.

"Hilda," she said. "She's the prize of them all. I met her in Holtville and asked her to move over here. She does social work, and the office is in Holtville. She has to go to the office, oh, every week or two; but most of her work is here. She was living in a little hotel where there was no one her age, nobody to talk to even; so she moved over here. We bought the record player secondhand from a dealer in Holtville, and we've had a million dollars worth of fun out of it."

"She spends most of her time working and being true to some oil boy in South America, of all places. She's no fun to go out with because she won't go, but just talking to her makes any problem easier; you'll see."

The music was strictly western or cowboy — "Way Out On the Prairie," and "Empty Saddles in the Old Corral," and, always, "Deep In The Heart Of Texas." Ophelia said Hilda had some Mexican records but that she did not care for them. Hilda had a stack of Mexican recordings we came to later. It seemed that the Mexican music and the western music were about equally divided.

Hilda came in about five-fifteen Sunday evening. She just walked in and said, "I got a letter from Carl. He thinks he's coming home for Christmas. I bought a new Chevy. I mean it's only two years old."

Hilda was tall and carrot-topped and not very good-looking. She was a big, Swedish-looking girl with freckles to match the carrot-top. I noticed that both her lipstick and fingernail polish matched the freckles and the hair. Her eyes looked as blue as her blue suit.

"How about taking a drive with me in my new car? You've had her all weekend and I want to get acquainted with her."

"I've had Bob most of the weekend, and I want to go to sleep," Ophelia said.

We drove a little way out of town to what they called the Dip. It was just off the highway, a washed out ditch. The wash-out must have occurred many years ago. It may once have been a little creek. It was completely hidden by one of those small mounds that dotted the area, called hills. There was a small clump of mesquites you had to almost bump into to get behind the mound into the dip. It was the only private place I ever found in Chaparral. It was important to so few people that it stayed private.

"I'm going to have to find somebody who will talk to me, or I'm going to have to leave town." I came right to the point. I told her the story of my few hours of life in Chaparral in detail, to this minute.

She just sat there thinking, and I began to wonder if she was going to let her mind show its real thoughts or give me some half-truths. Her freckles seemed to get deeper-hued as she considered the problem. Then she told me.

"Jennie, I've only been here a few months. Of course, I have already heard one version of your story as I came through the lobby. 'It was not your doing. The Mexican promoted the whole thing.' But I knew better. No Mexican would dare. Actually I brought you out here to see if you wanted to talk about it."

She paused for such a long time that I thought she was waiting for me to talk, but I had said it all.

"I went through all that the first month I was here," she finally said. "I've learned that you think what you want to, do what you want to, and say nothing about it. I can do a little good because of my job, and you will be able to do the same thing, but don't try to rush anything. It all comes so slowly, if ever. You'll never in a dozen years raise the social status of the Mexicans here. You may be able to do little things for individuals, but you're going about it wrong. They've hated them too long, ever since their ancestors took the cattle from across the river — stealing them — and also taking land on this side along the border. That's the way I hear it, anyway. You can know that, but don't say it. You can enjoy their music, but don't dance with them. You can enjoy their food, but don't eat with them. You can teach their children, but don't speak to them on the street. Never, never go into Little Mexico except to the schoolhouse. That is, if you want to avoid trouble here, you do it just this way. If anything a little off-color, or a lot off-

21

color ever happens here, you'd better assume, with the rest of Chaparral, that it was done by a Mexican. It's a perfect cover for the Anglos. No Anglo ever does anything wrong here."

I felt sick inside, raw and beaten. "It can't be possible. Why this is America, 1940 A.D., not the Middle Ages."

"I know exactly how you feel because I suffered, too, when I first came here. But, I decided I could do better work by keeping my eyes open and watching for opportunities to do little things."

"You're the first person who would talk to me and the first one who feels as I do. Is there anyone else?"

"Not that I know of, definitely. The preacher does what he can from the pulpit. Ophelia never says anything except 'leave it alone.' She just smiles and never comments. I think she must think that is the best way. What she really thinks I don't know. Lou never says anything, but Bert does the talking for them as you will learn. I guess that's all."

"It isn't all, Hilda."

"For me it is. Carl will be home, and we'll get married, and it will be the end of my working career. All I really want to be is a housewife, Jennie."

I went to sleep Sunday night thinking that nothing different could happen tomorrow. Well, something different, because I must begin to try to put into effect some of the theories of teaching I had learned in my year of college, but nothing else different could happen. I was at an impasse, but I was not finished with trying to learn the problem; I didn't know how futile would be the effort, and how surely I certainly was not through.

The telephone call came Monday morning.

"Miss Camish? Some of the mothers are here and want to know if they may come to school this morning with the children. It will be the first day for some of the little ones, and they are frightened."

"I thought parents always came to school the first day. Sure. I want them to. Don't they always?"

"Perhaps, in some places. Then it's agreeable with you if they bring the children?"

"Of course. Where are they?" The man sounded as if he

22

might have been the Mexican who was ordered out of Lee's.

"In Little Mexico, Miss Camish. We are *not* in *your* town."
He hung up.

At eight o'clock I started through the lobby to walk the
eight blocks to school. Lee was just walking out of the door
to go to the cafe.

"Where are you going so early?"

"To school."

"What for. You can drive it in a minute."

"I'm going to walk."

"Oh, no, you're not. I haven't been here long as you told
me, but no white woman walks to the Mexican section in
any town."

Cava came over and tried to get me to eat breakfast again.
Ophelia must have been sent for.

"Jennie," she said, "don't do it. You're fighting customs
that have been accepted here for a hundred years." Then, "Miss
Camish this is Mr. Falop." And I could never call him anything
but this last name, and often it came out Flip. He didn't like
it from this day.

"Ophelia told me about you," he said. "You kind of got off
on the wrong foot with that Meskin, didn't ye? Ha! Ha! Well,
don't worry none about it. We'll see that the story dies. Now get
in your car and go to school."

I did. There was nothing else I could do. Cava, Ophelia,
Lee, Flip and — from somewhere Bert had materialized — all
waiting to stop me if I took one more step. As I got into the
car Ophelia took a few steps backward as if to separate herself
from the group, and there was a drawn look of sadness on
her face. She must have felt very sorry for me that morning.
But I was not thinking of her. I was furious. Inside I was
seething with hatred of their lack of human understanding.

Halfway to the school was the little ditch, a washed-out
gully about a foot deep and three feet wide. Every September
the Mexican fathers filled it solidly with sand so that it
looked level for the new English teacher. But it blew out gradually until the ditch was there again, and you would have to stop
the car and ease over.

The English room was a large, square room that had been built

23

with hard-earned money. But with the Mexicans, it was a labor of love. They had built it to give their children a chance they had never had themselves. Here, the children learned only English. In the seven years they'd had the building not one teacher had stayed all of one year. So they started this year with this aim: to keep a teacher nine months. The children could be any age in the English room. The only requirement was that they were unable to speak English. When they learned enough English to start first grade work, they would get on the big red school bus and go to the public school in Holtville.

The mothers were standing beside the building, quietly, with little hands tightly clutching theirs. I counted eleven children and four mothers. One mother had two little ones, a boy and a girl, both trying desperately to hold to Mama's right hand as though she did not have a left one. They looked at me with huge, dark, frightened eyes as their mothers uttered soothing words of Spanish to them.

I smiled. They didn't. They clung more tightly to the hands. All except one boy who looked to be sixteen or seventeen years old. Such hatred and bitterness I had never before seen on a face of any age. I smiled, and he glared, face and body completely rigid.

I opened the door and asked them to come in. They looked at one lady; and when she nodded, they came in slowly, the little ones pulling back to keep from entering — the mothers urging them in, in cooing tones of love. One of the women was blonde, and I expected her to speak, but she just stood, defiant and sullen.

Then one of the mothers spoke.

"Teasher, I Miz Gomez. You say English. I say Spanish. I try to help you."

She was clean and neat and well-dressed in her inexpensive clothes. I knew she wanted to help her family.

Finally, the children had all been coaxed into their seats. There they sat, tense, clutching tablets and pencils, still imploring the mothers to take them home, pleading with their eyes, all except the big boy who slouched against the wall and glared, with his thumbs in the top of his pants. I smiled. He

24

glared. I asked him his name. Mrs. Gomez told me he was Pedro.

"I make you list," she said, and I gave her pencil and paper. All the mothers were there, except Pedro's.

The mothers stood along one wall of the room, silent and respectful, waiting to see what I would do. I did not know. I think I was more frightened of them and their children than they were of me. Mrs. Gomez may have sensed my perplexity. She said, "We go now," and they went, and I was glad.

Dear God, give me courage. Give me strength. Help me to help them. They need it more than some of Your poor mortals, Dear Lord. Help me to start right and help me to be a helper . . .

Aloud, I said, "Good morning. My name is Miss Camish. What is your name?"

I used all of the phrases I had been given in college to start a foreign language speaking group. I used the responses and tried to get them to repeat after me. There was no response. I tried pantomime, facial expressions, and a pleading voice. There was no response. I was doing it wrong. Somehow, regardless of the rule that said we speak only English in an American classroom, I had to learn a few Spanish words. I would say them on the playground, except I knew so few.

I walked from child to child touching each one lightly on the head or the shoulder. I smiled. They did not. Pedro continued to glare with cold hatred. When I patted the largest desk in the room, indicating he was to sit there, he said, "Naw," with complete denial. He stared at me all day long, never once removing his bitter eyes from my face. I could feel his eyes on my back as I wrote on the chalkboard.

One little girl started to cry, and I realized I had not shown them the bathrooms. I took them outside to the two lean-to type cubicles and showed them where to go. Pedro did not move. When we came back into the room, he seemed not to have changed his stance or his expression.

At eleven-thirty we all went to lunch. The children walked home, and I went to the hotel. We were off from eleven-thirty to one-thirty to have time for the siesta. Now, I would get some sewing done on my little secondhand portable sewing machine

25

and make my new piece of green gingham. I ate soup and milk and hurried in order to sew. The silence in the Vidaurri was as the silence on a lonely farm at two in the morning. I lay down on my bed.

I wonder who taught them to stand at attention when the teacher walks in or out of the room? I wonder why they stand and refuse to move until I walk out of the door first? I want them to go ahead and act like children. How can I get this across? How do I?

It was one-fifteen. When I arrived back at school the children were leaning against the outside of the building, sound asleep. Pedro was standing in the middle of the road, and I think he would have let me drive into him before he would have budged an inch. I contrived to miss him and laughed as if it were a joke. I went from child to child and gently touched each one and said, "Time for school."

They jumped up and stood there as if they had been caught in some wrongdoing. Pedro sauntered in fifteen minutes late and resumed his identical behavior of the morning. All afternoon we talked.

That is, I talked. I went over and over the same efforts of the morning and finally got two responses when school was out. Two little girls said, "Goot marnin' teasher." I was a complete failure my first day of teaching.

I sat and stared at the vacant desks and looked at my inability, my uselessness. I stared at a blank wall and began to understand why teachers never stayed. I reviewed the list Mrs. Gomez had made for me:

GOMEZ, Chacha — age 6 — girl
    Panchito — age 7 — boy
    Linda — age 8 — girl

GONZALES, Anna — age 6 — girl
    Leandro — age 8 — boy

GARCIA, Lupe — age 7 — girl
    Lucia — age 9 — girl
    Pedro — age 13 — boy

BURTON, Juanito — age 10 — boy

MORIN, Nina — age 6 — boy }
     Paula — age 6 — girl twins }

When I tried to remember where they had sat, I could only be sure about Pedro, because he had not sat. I think if I had never seen him again, I would have always seen him as he was our first day.

Back at the hotel I inquired of everybody I could find where I might be able to find someone to help me with Spanish so I could know just a little to get started. Although no one had ever seen her, it was mutually agreed that the wife of the Mexican Doctor would be the best one to teach me Spanish because she spoke the best English in Little Mexico. I never learned how so many people believed this, but I called her, in spite of Lee's "Go ahead. Call her if you want to waste your time learning that stupid lingo."

I did, so I called.

"Oh, no, Miss Camish. It is utterly impossible. You see, you could not come to my home, and I could not come to your hotel. In fact, I have never been in Chaparral, nor do I care to go there. We have never had an English teacher who wished to learn Spanish, though I think it commendable. If you really are interested . . ."

"Who could I get to help me?" As usual I got in deeper and wouldn't "leave it alone" as Perry said.

"The American High School Spanish teacher could perhaps be induced to tutor you. That is only a suggestion."

"But she doesn't teach the same Spanish my children speak. I want to learn how to talk to my mothers and the children. I want . . ."

"Miss Camish, your Spanish teacher speaks exactly the same Spanish that I do. I learned it at my home in Mexico. She learned it at one of your American colleges from an excellent professor whom I know well."

She hung up. Oh, Lord, let me do something right — just anything.

I wanted to meet this woman who probably had it all

27

over most of us in Chaparral, but who had too much pride and dignity to walk down our street. But I could see that I would never get the privilege. So, I picked up the telephone to call the high school teacher just as Hilda came in. I put it back in its cradle.

Hilda had cokes and peanuts. She opened the cokes, poured the peanuts in, and handed me one. There was a wild, happy look in her eyes, and I knew there was something on her mind. I wanted to tell her about my day at school, but I did not get to because she made a suggestion.

I like to remember that she made the suggestion — not I. I just fell in with the idea at once, and it was typical of everything I did: all wrong. This once, I like to remember that it was Hilda.

"Jennie, I — I — , ever since I've been here, I have wanted to go to Little Mexico at night. I want to see what they do. I want to walk. Now, more than ever, since they threw that scene when you wanted to walk to school this morning. And, to be honest, I never before knew anybody I thought might go with me. Will you go?"

I had my coat on, and she continued talking as we walked out the door.

"I don't want to ride. I want to walk. They dance over there every night, and they say it is the roughest place north of the border. It has a terrible reputation, in Chaparral that is, and I just want to see. You're supposed to go in a car with a man, and to Lee's, when you want to dance. Me, I want to go to what they call the dance palace. I don't believe all I hear, and I want to see. I've thought of it all day. Are you game?"

"We're three blocks from the hotel, going in that direction. I grabbed my coat and beat you out the door, and you ask if I'm game."

It was dark now. The low hills behind the business district were outlined in pale silhouette, fading rapidly into darkness. The road was dusty, narrow, winding and enclosed on either side by weeds and sparse desert growth. The soft dust crept up until you could feel it all the way to your hair. It clung tightly. We walked slowly and quietly. I remember that we did not say anything until we stepped onto the piece of ground where the

28

ditch had been filled. She stopped, just stood there, with one foot on the sand and one foot on the hard-packed earth beside it. In the last of the daylight her hair looked like old burgundy, and her voice sounded misty, wondering and far away. I could not see her eyes.

THREE

feet across and one foot deep and it's as wide and deep as the Rio Grande. O. K. Let's cross it," she said as though we had to plunge for our lives.

Right there the Mexican shacks started. We passed the school, continued along the narrow, curving, dusty road and up the hill. Built into the sides of the hills were the little houses, sand-colored and looking like projections of the hills themselves. There were one-, two- and sometimes three-room houses, adobe, going out not up, and looking as if they had been there throughout the life of the hill.

"Who lives in that big white house?"

"The doctor. There's a new building, nice looking. I never saw it before. I don't know who lives there. I haven't had an assignment here since I moved to the Vidaurri, if that means anything. I just thought of it."

We could faintly hear the music before we crossed the ditch. Now, it became louder and louder, and now it was very loud. We were halfway up the hill.

The structure was half in the hill and half dangling over. It had no top and only a floor with board railings on three sides. The fourth side was the hill. On the side next to the hill, vines that had been planted and carefully watered climbed and trailed down onto the floor. The center of the town's social life was the dance palace.

30

They danced under the stars, or moon, or dark clouds — in the rain. The same three-piece orchestra was playing the same music. The floor was crowded with people trying to stomp through it. They were delirious with joy.

"Esa es la profesora. Esa es la profesora. Mama, Mama."

Thus was our presence announced. Gradually the music and dancing stopped, and the couples became very quiet. Then Chacha's mama discovered we had no husbands, and she took on the role of protector. She plied us with little cakes and pralines and water. Nobody asked us to dance. Nobody looked at us after the first shock.

"Hilda, that's the Mexican fellow I told you about in the cafe. The one with that pretty little girl with the roses in her hair."

"Those are not roses. They're paper flowers. They all wear them after the zinnias wilt. I never saw that man before. He must be new here."

Then, he saw me, I think. He looked above, below and beyond me. He didn't look at me. He did not miss a beat in his rhythm.

"He doesn't stomp. He just dances — like Perry. He has shoes on."

I had on my pale pink cotton dress. I wanted a pink paper rose for my hair, and I wanted to dance with him. I began to feel sick, and I was reeling and twirling, going down and calling Hilda. Somebody screamed, and then I heard the din of screams and felt my own screams. Hilda was going up — away beyond me. Then, it was quiet and black — black and very lonely.

I saw the wall first. I was lying facing it. It was a soft, warm brown. I looked down to the multicolored spread over me and felt the pain in my ankle, hot and throbbing.

"Miss Smaltz, she is awake now. She is all right. She is only afraid, but the pain is little. She will sleep now with the sedative."

Then, the voice said, "But we have to get her back to the hotel," and I recognized Hilda.

"That I forbid," the doctor said. "She must stay off the foot tonight. Tonight, yes, but tomorrow take her to your own doctor in Chaparral."

Hilda said, "Everybody knew what was happening but you. The dance floor just folded up, fell to the ground and rolled down the hill piece by piece, and you . . . you fainted." She sounded disgusted.

"What's the matter with my foot?"

"You sprained your ankle, but you're going to live. You went through the floor. I scrambled up the hill before my section fell . . . but you . . . Oh, no. You passed out."

"Where are we?"

"You're fine. Just shut up and let the shot take effect. We have to get you to the hotel."

Half awake, I took stock of my surroundings. The room was large and square, with low ceilings and quite colorful: browns and reds and greens with some orange. Perfect harmony here. I saw the record player and realized I had been hearing it all along.

Hilda said, "Play 'Cielito Lindo' again, and maybe she'll sleep."

I was again coming out of a deep narcotic sleep. My foot felt dead. Hilda was talking.

"Now, listen. I don't like it any more than you do, but I have to get her to the hotel. We didn't ask for this."

"Oh, yes, you did ask for this. Why didn't you stay on the other side of the ditch? You know the rules. She didn't . . . and she's sure going to too much trouble to learn. But I brought her here. Now, let's think what to do about it." Then he added, "I'll go down and get some coffee. What would you like to eat?"

The soft, slightly bitter voice had a lulling quality I wanted to listen to. Tired and concerned and somehow defeated — not angry. I just wanted to stay here. I had never been so comfortable and relaxed in my life.

Hilda said, "Jennie, are you awake? You feel like talking a little?"

"Who were you talking to?" I asked.

"Jennie, you know who lives in that new building we saw? Well, we're in it. I mean we're in this new building, and we must get out of it." Then she whispered, "Jennie, that Mexican who tried to buy the ham sandwich lives here."

She should not have said it. I knew I would see to it that they had a hard time getting me out of here.

"What's his name?"

"Juan Ortega."

I repeated it over and over to myself, dreamily. Even with my mispronunciation, it sounded like music.

He came back from downstairs with coffee; and when Hilda introduced us, the effect of the narcotic was gone though I had been playing it for all it was worth. Something stronger filled the room. It took away the hurt in my ankle. I looked at him with my soul in my eyes, I hoped, but nothing at all happened to his face. There was no change in him in any way. I knew I wanted to spend the night here and that I would have to pretend to be very ill. Somehow, I wanted to get him to tell me about himself. Tomorrow? There was no tomorrow. There was only this night.

Hilda had argued or discussed with Juan for three hours how to get me out of there. Almost, she had reached the limit of her endurance. She tried again.

"What are we going to do?"

"I'll call a girl I know and have her drive you to the hotel. Get your car and come back here for Miss Camish. Cava can take her in the back entrance."

"Don't be unreasonable. Just take us home."

"We both know that won't work. You know you can't afford to be seen with me."

They could talk forever if they liked. I intended to stay here and solve somthing or get involved. Whatever it was, I wanted to stay here. My ankle did not hurt. I did not hurt anywhere, but I moaned as if I were in terrible pain. They talked and talked, and Hilda finally gave up at one o'clock in the morning. She went into the bedroom and went to sleep. I was alone with Juan! My hands ached to touch him. I tried to sit up; he tried to force my swollen foot into my shoe; he could not. Even if you walk to Little Mexico unescorted, you don't walk to the Vidaurri at one in the morning alone. I wanted to run my fingers through his blue-black hair, and so I did.

Later we went down through his cafe, on the first floor, and

33

Hilda and I got into his new red Buick. Everything he owned seemed to be new — his business, apartment, furniture, car, and even his clothes. He drove us to the alley behind the Vidaurri, put us in the service elevator and said, "Miss Camish: please stay on this side of the ditch. This is your side. Can't you understand? Don't ever again come over there except to teach the children. Promise me this, please. It's the widest river you'll ever cross, and you'll have so many years to regret it.

"I'll see you again, Juan," I said. "Some way, I'll see you again."

Gradually waking early in the morning, just as the purple shadows turned to gold, I remembered that time alone with Juan. The record player was softly playing Mexican music, and he kept changing it. The night was very quiet and still. Little Mexico was sound asleep, just as though its social world had not tumbled down the hill. They would build another one, and until then they would dance in the street if they felt like it. I could see across the room and beyond the couch and out the window. The moonlight was casting strange dark shadows on the low, rolling hills in the distance. It was little different than the view from my hotel window, but this view would be etched on my brain, always. It was somehow different — different to anything I would ever see.

"It's almost morning," I said.

He looked through the window.

Then I said, "This is a lovely room."

And he replied. "It's pure Mexican: colors, motif, and mood, exactly as I like to spend my time, in here. Isn't it garish and vulgar and overly bright to you? Go on, tell the truth. It's poorly-planned Mexican hodgepodge. Oh, I've heard it all. But, I love it, and whatever you think won't change it."

Then he added, "It's past time you should go back to the hotel. Here are your shoes," and I could not put the shoe on either. I did not try very hard. I just moaned about how it hurt.

My foot and ankle were tightly bandaged I discovered that morning, but I could walk.

"What on earth happened to you?" Lee asked.

I told her the lie we had planned: that I had stumbled on the street and we put the bandage on. The bandage was a professional-looking job, but nobody ever questioned it. The lie was good practice. I was to tell it many times.

Lee said, "I just took a long walk before I have to go to work. I love the early morning, don't you? I walked toward Little Mexico, not there, of course, but in that direction. It was black as pitch from here except for one tiny light that burned on the top of the hill. Somebody must have been sick. They don't stay up all night with the light on. Well, I gotta go."

Hilda said, "We must get you to school. You can walk all right. I'll drive you down if you don't feel like driving your car. The thing is, you must be there as if nothing had happened. Did Lee believe you, do you think?"

"No, she probably saw it all from right there. Everybody in Chaparral will know . . . "

"I think not, Jennie. She was only interested in her little early-morning walk. She didn't really pay any attention. I hate the lie. I hate to lie, but there is no other way. Lee didn't even ask you where you had been. If she thinks we've been out with some ranchers, that's O.K. Just don't stay out with an oil boy."

"How about a Mexican?" I asked.

She said, "Don't mention that even to me. If we let it slip once, we're in some real trouble."

"But, Hilda, they are bound to find out about it."

"No, they won't. Nobody saw us, not even Cava. Even if they knew it, they wouldn't believe it."

"How did I get into that house?"

"He carried you to his car, with me running along behind, and took you there. Don't you even remember that?"

I did not, but I wished that I did.

"He ran over everybody getting to you; didn't pay any attention to me, or to that girl he was with, just walked over everybody. At his apartment he called the doctor, and you know the rest of it."

Yes. I knew the rest of it.

At school the children ignored my bandage, ignored the fact that I had been there the previous night, and began to talk a little — a few words in English. They sang "Blue Eyes, I'll Never

Love Brown Eyes Again" to me in Spanish. So many times I was to be so depressed, I thought I had lost all hope and these children could give me new hope. Tentative smiles, feeble attempts at English, and Pedro walked in and sat down. He slouched and kept his feet in the aisle all day and said nothing, but he sat down.

It was a long day. As I came in the hotel lobby after school Falop was explaining the accident.

"No. Nobody was hurt. Just a typical Mexican accident. You know they live in their dumps till they fall down and . . ."

Bert said, "How's the foot, Jennie?"

"Oh, fine."

"Too bad you had that accident first week here. Glad you can walk. The city needs to fix that hole. It's bad for business. Everybody in Chaparral is going to wind up with a broken leg if something isn't done about that big hole."

Falop came in with, "Come outside Jennie. Now, show us just how you fell in that hole. Yes, that's the way I told Bert it happened. You could sue the city for that, Jennie. If you will, we will all go along with you. Been trying to get that hole filled in for years."

If they had been trying to fill in that hole, it would have taken one man perhaps ten minutes with a shovel. They tried to get me to force my sore foot into it, and Ophelia could not even have got *her* foot in it. They must have known where I had been. They knew I could not have been injured in that little hole.

"Almost had your rear wheel in it, too, and . . ."

Hilda came up in time to save me.

The hotel was very quiet that night so we sat in the lobby and listened to keep from facing our lie.

Falop said, "Guess the ranchers took that oil boy good Saturday night. Guess these oil boys never learn."

After hearing a long tirade on the virtues of the ranchers and evils of the oil boys, Hilda and I went up to my room.

"Hilda, my little ones know. Even Pedro sat down, and it's only the second day of school. They would smile and touch my arm and look up shyly at me. They knew, but never by word or gesture did they indicate it. Some of the fright had left their eyes, and I had learned to say, 'Good morning, what is your name?' in Spanish."

"You did, huh?"

There was never anything in the paper; but after last night, we bought the paper, and the headlines hit me in the pit of my stomach.

MURDER IN LITTLE MEXICO

Some time last night a nineteen-year old Mexican boy was shot in the back and killed in Little Mexico. The shooting occurred in the vicinity of the dance palace (see column 3). The dance palace fell down the hill last night, with people screaming and lumber falling. The shot was not heard that we can determine, mainly due to the noise of the screams and falling lumber. Citizens of Chaparral can rest assured that the killer will be apprehended. The police department urges that no persons from Chaparral go to Little Mexico unless absolutely necessary. Guards will be placed around all possible exits and areas. The English classroom will be open as usual according to our information.

We were too stunned to speak for some minutes. I spoke first.

"Of course, they must guard anything that has a Mexican around. You watch them pin this on a Mexican without even an investigation." I think there I began a deep anger that was to continue to grow.

Hilda said, "Let's walk."

We went to the little park. Ophelia and Hank were sitting on the bench under the tree beside the zinnias where Perry and I had sat just three nights ago. Hank was talking. They did not see us.

"I can give you everything you ever wanted."

We got into Hilda's car and went to the dip and parked behind the mesquites. We could see pale lights in Little Mexico but none on the top of the hill.

With no preamble I asked, "What if they do question everybody who was at the dance palace?"

"They will, they think. They will never know we were there. Never in a million years will the children tell that their teacher was there. Jennie, you don't know them yet. You don't know what you could mean to them. That's not what worries me. Somebody was killed in that spot during the time you were pulling the faint, and there was so much noise nobody could have heard a gun."

"We lied, and I've never had to do that before."

"Well, you have to now, and do stop worrying."

"I want to go home."

"That's a coward's way out and not like you. I couldn't *drive* you out of this, and you know it."

"I guess not. They will pin it on the Mexican, and I want to be here when they doll it up for the paper."

The "guards" were all over Little Mexico and Chaparral. The little ones still acted as if nothing had happened. Pedro was not there.

The police who visited me made a speech. He came into the room and called me out, and you could feel the fear and panic in the children. Their eyes followed me as if they wanted to protect me if they dared.

"We know that somebody was killed just across the road and up the hill last night, but now, Miss Camish, I don't want you to get panicky. You will be protected every minute you are here. If there was any danger in your classroom being open, it would not *be* open. A member of the police force will be on call all the time that you are here. Don't let the children talk about the murder."

"I was there. I can tell you . . . "

"Well, we know, of course. You would naturally be nervous, but now let's just . . . "

"But I was there. I mean the dance palace just . . . "

"Now, Miss Camish, we intend to get to the bottom of this, and we know you like the Mexicans, but we don't want no made-up tales."

"But, please listen. I was there —

"You'd better dismiss early and go on back to the hotel. You won't be so upset." And he was gone.

Cava was telling Hilda as I walked into the hotel, "Miss

Smaltz, somebody, some place way off in South America is a callin' ye. You ask foah operata fouh, an' she tell you."

Hilda could hardly talk. Between long pauses she said, "Carl, Honey . . . Oh, Carl . . . Give me that date again and the time . . . and . . . and . . . I love you."

She turned from the telephone like a sleepwalker and said, "He will be here on December 22, right here in the Vidaurri, and I don't believe it."

The Mexican incident took a back seat with Hilda and a back seat in the paper. Daily, in print and in person, the police told us they would find the murderer and that is all.

We listened to Falop in Lou's apartment.

"I betcha ten police already got the murderer. They always get 'em. Beats me how the Mexicans think they can go around killing each other and get by with it."

"How do you know it was a Mexican?" I asked.

"Let's not talk about it tonight, Honey," Ophelia said as if it were not important.

It was all there was to talk about, and it continued. Bert, in his dignity, Falop in his fury, Lee in her bitterness, Ophelia with sweetness and light and only Hilda and I with fury matching Falop's. Ophelia had her mind on Bob. Hilda's thoughts were of Carl, and I went to school the next day feeling sick both physically and mentally — so sore I felt as though I had been beaten. I knew as surely as I was an Anglo that this murder would eventualy be attributed to a Mexican, and probably one with a large family to support.

I tried to write lesson plans, but I kept seeing their tender smiles and their half-frightened big, soft eyes long after they had gone. Pedro's vacant seat stood alone. In my attempt at planning and in my grief this came out: What is a Mexican? A member of mestizo parentage. Yes, but so far as is known, he came into being when Spain conquered Mexico and the Spanish inter-married with the Aztec Indians. I am French, English and Scotch-Irish that I know of. There may be other bloods in me. Am I not a mestizo? We are all Americans. My little ones, all of us in Texas, are Americans regardless of which side of the river the accident of birth may have placed us. So, why are my Mexi-cans plotted against? I think about these things as I wonder what

I can do for you.

Pedro, with your deep hatred in your eyes, is it for me or for all Anglos? What happened to do this to you? How can I reach you? I must learn how to help you. Don't hate me, Pedro. I do so want you to love me and let me be your friend.

Lupe and Lucia, you look so much alike, you might be twins — quiet, calm, with all the stoicism of the Indian, along with dirty clothes and dirty little bodies. How I long to clean you up and see you smile and see you love life.

Nino and Paula, blue eyes and black hair and yet you look nothing alike. You look as though you do not know why you are here, and you do not like being here. Come to me, and let us be friends. How I do want you to understand me.

Chacha, you sit there all day long, deeply engrossed in learning to write the strange English words. You are beginning to read a few words in your lovely Spanish accent. I smile, but you don't return the smile. A sort of wistful, tentative look tells me you may like me; someday you may learn to love me.

Anna, do you understand in any way at all how I feel? You, with your reserved manner, slanty black eyes and straight black hair, might have stepped straight out of the old Japan. Today, you said "Goot pie, teasher," and ran. That is good.

Panchito, in appearance and manners and mannerisms, you are pure Anglo. Yet, your mother and father are wholly Spanish. What ancestor gave you the *blue eyes* and the *blonde* hair. Was he *French* like mine?

Leandro, you look pure Spanish, as if your ancestors might all have been Spanish. You look like that, but you act all Indian, with your expressionless eyes and your never-changing face.

Linda, why do you cry when I try to talk to you? Are you afraid of me only because I am blonde? Do you want your mama only because you are little? Grey eyes and brown hair, you do not look, in color even, like any of the others.

Juanito, I have a very special place for you because to date you are the only child who has said to me, "Teasher, I luf you," and for no reason that I know.

All of this, and the Anglos tell me, "Oh, some Mexican. I don't know. They all look alike, you know."

No two of you look alike. Why don't you wear your lovely

Mexican clothes and leave your heavy, blueish hair straight and lovely as God made it? What have we done to you? Did we do it? Are you proud to be a Mexican? Proud of your race? Why don't you trust me? What can I do? Is your pride of race real, or is it a false, bitter pride? Do you dislike me because I am *rubia?* I can no more prevent that than you can prevent being a brunette. I hope you are proud of the blood that runs in your veins. I am proud of mine, and it, too, is composed of many nationalities and many peoples of many thousands of years — too far back for the understanding.

If I could have my wish I would do for you these things: help you keep the courtesy, protocol, and culture of the Spanish; the quiet dignity and pride of the Indian; the will to fight for survival and betterment of the Negro; and the ambition to be somebody of all the past and present Asiatic peoples. I would teach you to appreciate the many freedoms of America. I would teach you the meaning of democracy, of Americanism, of free enterprise and try to give you the ambition to succeed and to know that success constitutes many things, the least of which is financial gain. I would teach you the meaning of progress and peace of mind and the goodness in kindness, and the happiness in understanding. I would have you keep the good of the past culture as you add the good of the new culture. I would continue to teach you English; I would have you see how hard I try to learn your language. I would have you try harder to learn mine. I would give you all these things; and, finally, I would give you two grand prizes: pride of your race and of Mexico, and pride of America.

How would I do this? How do you make lesson plans for this? How? With the help of God and the help of your understanding: Oh, how I am going to need both!

FOUR

was having a great time back at the hotel, discussing the Mexicans. He said they were animals, savages, usually stab 'em to death, but this was an odd one. He had used a gun. Argument over a woman probably.

"Good thing it wasn't a white man who got killed. Every man in Chaparral and for a several hundred-mile radius would be here to tear that little town apart."

I could see that Bert was enjoying this talk. We were sitting around in the big chairs in the lobby when Lou suggested that we go to their apartment for coffee.

"Traveling around we used to drink B and B after dinner. That's bourbon and brandy, you know. We'd have a martini before dinner. Here I've found out you drink everything straight, and it makes no difference what time it is, or whether you eat or not."

Falop laughed loudly and got no response.

Ophelia said, "Who drinks here, Mr. Falop? I know very few people who drink."

I wondered what was happening to Ophelia. This was her boss and she loved her job, and the whole town liked her. Falop did not answer.

Ophelia walked out, and I walked out behind her. I would like to know this girl. We went to her room. She said that she had been here ever since she could remember — that she had no

42

people that she knew of, that she lived with a couple on a ranch who had since died and that she came to town to work, and that was all. She may have thought she was telling me about herself, but she told nothing. Just that, and then, I asked her how she felt about the Mexicans. She told me: she felt that God made us all equal, that she felt nothing deeply for either race as a race, but that she just loved people. She explained to me that I was making a mistake in making an issue of a situation I could do nothing about, and that I would be happier and get along better if I could just accept it and not talk about it. She seemed to feel nothing at all and, again, she had told me nothing.

But she got along this way. Everybody remembered her from grade school and they were all vague about where she came from . . . if they ever knew. She was always the same, said nothing against anybody, and everybody seemed to love her. She was very calm, and nothing seemed to bother her; but I thought I had heard her crying once in the night. I was not sure. Then, she suddenly switched to music. She put western music on the phonograph. She had talked to me, but she never seemed to have let me know her.

Hilda came in from listening downstairs to Falop and Bert and started talking. She thought she had figured out why Lou, and Bert always went to Mexico. She had thought, when she first met them, that they had been all over the world. They had money. This was understood, but never proved. Why didn't they travel? They go to Mexico so they can find something to hate. They could hate enough here, but they go to Mexico and come back criticizing everything they can find. They vent their superiority on the Mexicans, and that makes them feel good. They must have really been talking about the Mexicans to have Hilda so upset. Something in their pasts nobody knew, she said. I guess it's the only way they can feel superior. Lou is so quiet about it, and Bert is so dignified; yet they despise them, I think. Nobody seems to know where Lou and Bert came from, and you would hear they got their money in oil, or they made it in Mexico. Nobody knew what they actually did. It seemed unlikely that Bert had always managed a hotel, even though he said he had. He did not manage this one. Cava did.

Hilda said, "Jennie, let's go out to the ditch and watch the moon come up. We'll go crazy if we just sit around here and talk about this."

Listening to Hilda's story was an interesting change. It took my mind off my children and my poor, beaten Mexicans for a little while. Hilda did not decide to be a social worker. It just happened. She planned to be a school teacher and had one year of college in that field. Her parents died when she was a baby, and a sister old enough to be her mother raised her. Before she was born, her grandparents, together with her family, moved to a farm near Fredericksburg. This was during World War I when they were all looked down on because they spoke German.

Hilda did not speak German. That had been forbidden in her home before she was born. Mostly what Hilda knew about her past was what she had been told. After one year in college on a scholarship, she had gone to work on the family farm. This was the first salaried job she had found.

Carl lived on the adjoining farm. He grew up there. He speaks German although he is Swedish, and Hilda used to tell him she was glad they stopped speaking German in her family for she would never have learned it. Carl signed a two-year contract with this oil company in South America and was sending her every dime he could spare, and she was saving all of it. They planned to make a down payment on a farm of their own. No, she had not wanted to go with him, and he had wanted her to. They were going to have something some day, and this way they could get a start.

"I don't know whether Carl is good-looking or what, Jennie. He's — well, he's tall and sort of your color, and . . . well, he's Carl. I can't imagine ever marrying anyone else. I never would, no matter what happens."

"You're too young to talk like that, even though nothing is going to happen."

"I mean I couldn't, Jennie. It wouldn't be right. I mean I wouldn't want to."

In my room Ophelia said, "I wish Bob could let me know when he's here what weekend he'll be back. Now, I'll have to break a date with Hank, and he won't like that. Funny, he said

44

Perry would call you, but they never do that. Always, just one calls."

"Why do you go with Hank? You don't care anything about him really, do you?"

"No," she said. "I guess not. I really care nothing about anybody but Bob, but he comes when it's convenient for him, not for me. I'm not engaged to Bob. I'll tell him I'm going out. In fact, I've never made him any promises, and I'm tired of sitting here. Every weekend I sit and know how much fun they are having at Lee's."

"Well, it can be fun to sit up here and think what hangovers a few of them may have the next day," I said.

"Well, I will break a date with Hank, and then I'll tell Bob this time. I'll call the ranch right now, tonight."

While she was calling the ranch, I got the telephone call from Perry.

"Listen, Hon," he said, "you stay right there in the hotel. Don't leave your room. I'll be there soon as I can get there. Don't even go down in the lobby. Keep Hilda with you, but don't leave your room!"

Like everything else that was happening to me, it did not make sense. Ophelia had called the ranch about tonight. Bob had called her hours ago. Perry had just called me. They could not possibly get here tonight.

I went to my room to be alone. I was completely spent. I felt sore in body and mind. Hilda was doing everything in the world that she could to keep my mind off the Mexican situation, but eternally it stayed there, right on top of my mind, on top of anything else that was discussed.

Hilda came in, sat on the edge of my bed, and started talking.

"There are four classes of people in the cattle country, Jennie, and never in your lifetime will you change any of them: the millionaires, the Mexicans, the people who work in town, and the teacher. Their ancestors, some time way back, staked a claim for so many sections of land. Some of them lived all of their lives and never saw all of it. That is, I hear this. The story goes that some great-grandfathers, oh, years back, staked the claim and stole a few cattle, or whatever was walking around across the river, and they were in business. You know the Rio Grande

45

is dry most of the time unless there is a flood, and that's almost never. I think they must have just walked the cattle across the river. Some of them may have traded or even brought their starting herds. I really don't know. But I guess it was unusual. Well, they added to their herds and their outbuildings, then they died and left it. The next generation added to and improved, and they took their wives out of dug outs and put them in adobe shacks. Each generation kept adding to and building improvements until you see homes and setups like the Holt Ranch. And every generation thinks they did it all themselves, or that's what they want to think. They don't want to remember that it cost them nothing. So, it's their divine right to set the pace for everything — which church to attend, or what they all wear."

So far, I loved the speech, but did they all have homes like that? Hilda said they did not. Not the cowboys who worked for the ranchers. Most of them did not have homes. Even the ones who work for the big ranchers may have a few thousand acres of land and a few hundred head of cattle. They live in bunkhouses, or they build houses, and to us even they are big money.

At the opposite end of the scale are the Mexicans. They have nothing, nothing at all. I don't know how they get enough to eat. They all get paid, but not enough to support a family.

The working people — I think all other people feel about them as Ophelia says she does about the Anglo-Mexican situation — nothing at all. I don't believe Ophelia feels that way. You have to feel something, don't you?

Where did Hilda learn all this in so short a time?

Ophelia had explained it all to her in almost these words. Ophelia had been here most of her life and she told Hilda the same little nothings she had told me about her past.

"The teacher, Jennie, you don't know what you mean to them. You're like a missionary. If only they can get you to stay. One never stays."

"I don't know anything about Juan," I said. "Who is he? Where did he come from? Why did he come here? He's not putting out any information, but for some reason he must have decided to come here . . ."

How I wanted to talk to her. How I wanted to know more! I said, "I'm going to start home-visits next week. I guess that

46

will be reason for gossip, but I'm going into their homes if the parents will let me. I have only five families represented in my room, and I'm going to learn all I can about these children if they will let me in."

She laughingly reminded me that the doctor's wife would not let me in. But I believed that Mrs. Gomez would, and I determined to start from there. The first thing — the main thing — I wanted to do was learn something about Pedro. He sat in the seat and then he had not been back to school — since the dance palace fell.

"Well, there's a breakdown on Carl, life in Chaparral, and that leaves my job. I might as well finish, then I will have told you all I know about me," Hilda said. "I do various things. Some of them have nothing to do with social work. Most of my work is welfare work in Little Mexico, or in the Mexican section in Holtville with people who need financial, medical, or other help. But, because of my not being certified, I'm limited. I don't know how I got this job. I had good grades in sociology, and I had my background. You see, I was once a member of a minority race, and the feeling for the job is there. I don't know, exactly, how I got this job, but I love it. I can do very little, and that's what I wish you could see. You, also, can do very little. But you can help if you sort of shut up, listen and look. I'm not allowed to see the psychologist's case records. Really, it's only one case which is not in my field at all and he tells me what he wants me to know.

"There is a private mental institution right in Holtville. It's just a big white house with no signs on it but that's what it is. It is called a rest home. They have a doctor, nurses, a psychologist and call in a psychiatrist when they need one. They have very few patients, the rules are not rigid, and they have more freedom than they have in a state institution. Of course, the inmates are closely watched, but they are made to feel that they are not watched, if you know what I mean. It's more like a nice private home: music, movies, books, really nice. Usually, they don't take seriously ill patients there, but they do have one patient who was diagnosed as suffering from anxiety and tension. She has become worse. I don't know what they are going to do about her or what they call her illness now.

47

"The oddest thing is that she despises men and loses confidence in any woman after the first visit. Yet, since June the first, she has welcomed me. Nobody knows why. The nurses asked me to go to the home with her, and the first time I went this woman called me in from the hall. She called me Gertrude and asked about the children. Nobody knows who Gertrude is, but then the woman is likely to call me anything.

"The doctor can listen in without her being aware of it, and she will go a week without talking. Then, someone will call me, and she will talk. She has become very important to me, like a close friend; and I'd give anything if I could help her. She's the loveliest thing. From the back she looks like Ophelia except that her hair is long, too heavy, and almost blonde. She is built like Ophelia and walks like her — you know — proud. She has big blue, vacant eyes. If her eyes didn't look so vacant, you would only notice how pretty she is.

"I don't know what the doctor can get from hearing her talk to me; I just listen and if she stops I ask a question.

"She gets furious with me when I don't call her the name she has in mind for that particular day. She has called herself 'Talooloo-Taloo-Toolee' and sometimes Toolie, so we all call her Toolie. I don't know her name, unless it is Tulia; that is what the psychiatrist calls her.

"No, really, I know almost nothing about her. The doctor did tell me she is only twenty-six years old, has five children, one husband, and one brother. That is all. She talks about other people; but as far as they know, there are none. She calls her husband 'Po' or 'Porter' and sometimes even 'Portellis.' Her brother is Bo or Borter or Bortellis. She has a sort of fixation about names. She makes up peculiar names and then laughs as though they sounded clever. She asks about Bobby every time I see her, and I'm to say he's much better. This is one of her children who has epileptic attacks. Sometimes she's furious at her brother when he doesn't come to see her when she thinks he should. She is always furious at her husband. He hasn't been there since May, and the doctor said he had been devoted for the almost a year that she has been there. At first, he paid all the bills, came often, and she was getting better. He could take her out to eat sometimes, and about a month before he stopped coming he took her home for a weekend. Then, he suddenly dropped out of sight. The doctor says they were very much in love and that her husband did all he could for her.

"Yes, I've asked him why and he says he would rather not tell me why the husband does not come anymore."

When she paused I wanted to hear more. I had been living this sad story and I asked, "Does her Bobby still have attacks?"

"Oh, yes. He gets worse. The children are in a private home, and the doctor did tell me the brother was paying the bills now."

"Hilda, I know why they won't tell you everything."

"They have their reasons."

"You're telling *me,* and I think you're not supposed to tell any of this."

Gradually, a look of understanding spread over her face, and she said, "Yes, you may be right. You see, I can't tell anything I shouldn't because I don't really know anything to tell." Then she added, "Last time I was there, she let me shampoo her hair. It hadn't been done in a month. She wouldn't let the beauty operator touch her."

There was a slight pause, then Hilda continued, "Now, she wants to kill her brother. 'Did I tell you,' she asked me very calmly, 'I think I'll shoot him?' I really get upset sometimes, but I have to go when they call, even though she makes no sense. She's not really unhappy. She thinks she lives in a pretty nice hotel and talks about the good service."

"Hilda," I asked, "could you find out, in your office in Holtville, anything about Juan? I mean, if he has done something wrong or anything?"

She looked whipped. "Jennie, I've talked everything under the sun to get your mind off that night, and I don't know what else to say. I can tell you this; you can't go on this way. You'll crack up, Jennie. And Jennie did you ever see anybody who really cracked up? I mean really? We talk about it, but I mean really? It's a thing you never forget. And it's something one never completely gets over. There is always the fear of falling apart again. I'm serious, Jennie. You're hurting yourself, and I think I couldn't stand it if you went to pieces.

It was late and I was tired and sleepy, but I knew I could not sleep.

"Jennie, this woman was once just a girl like us. There was nothing wrong with her except the doctor thinks she had babies too fast. But there is something on her mind. Something she couldn't cope with. You have to compromise somewhere, Jennie, or go under. You can't go on like this."

Ophelia was crying when we went in. We knew it this time, and we both went to her room. She told us Bob had called and said he and Perry couldn't get here until tomorrow. I thought tomorrow would be soon enough since it was eleven o'clock anyway. Ophelia was incoherent. She said she was going to call Hank and tell him to come on in. Why? Ophelia did not have to go out every Saturday night. Her shop had just been closed, and once she had not thought of dating afterwards. Now, she had received a telephone call and she had gone to her room to cry.

I wondered if perhaps we would both go to pieces. I knew my problems. I did not know Ophelia's. Hilda seemed to have none. She could handle any situation that came her way. For the first time I realized what Hilda had been trying to tell me. She had been trying to help me by telling me these stories that had nothing to do with us, or with our lives, so I would not get involved. But something was already happening to me. I was twenty years old and my shoulders were very old, tight and hard and tense. Somehow, I couldn't let anything happen to me. I had to help my Mexicans. I could not sleep.

As I lay wide-eyed, I determined to see all of my parents who would let me in the next week. That was the only decision I could reach as I went cold and hot, over and over, reliving a murder that was getting farther over in the corner of the front-page daily, but was still on the front page. It was a daily repetition with hints that the police knew who the killer was and that he was expected to give himself up since they knew. I knew this was a threat. If they could have pinned it on any Mexican at all, on any pretext at all, it would have been done.

After church and after lunch, we were standing around in the lobby. Ophelia was watching the clock intently, as if she could speed it up. Her voice sounded as if it might stop. She had had a difficult time singing the solo part in the choir. Brother Way seemed to be watching her all during the service. Hilda and I were watching her now. Did Bob mean this much to her? Did she know where he was? Why he was not here?

She sat and watched. Then we went on up to her room for our siesta. Lee came in, just off duty, stood in the center of my room and looked all around.

"This is the cleanest room in the hotel besides Ophelia's They even take the coke bottles down . . . clean it up every day like spring cleaning. They always cleaned Ophelia's room that way. Now yours. Mine looks like it got a lick and a promise. I don't get it."

Hilda asked, "Don't you, Lee?"

"No, I don't. The cleaning women are Mexican, of course, and they clean our rooms when we are out. I know why Jennie's room is so clean. She loves Mexicans. But I never have figured out why Ophelia's room gets such good treatment. She leaves them alone, and they keep her room spotless."

Lee went to her room. Hilda went to sleep. I went down to the lobby to go — I did not know where. Ophelia's eyes were still glued to the clock. She was idly flipping the pages of a magazine.

Outside, I got into the car and started driving. When I saw Pedro walking down the middle of the powdery, dusty road, hands in pockets, head down, kicking up dust swirls with his bare feet, I realized I had driven to Little Mexico. If he heard the car, he gave no indication of it. I think he would, once again, have let me drive into him before giving way. I thought I would try again to make friends with him.

I asked him to get into the car. After a long hesitation, he did, but silently, slowly and sullenly. He sat hugging the door, trying to braid the toes of one bare foot into the toes of the other bare foot. At the same time he kept his hands over the holes in the knees of his jeans. He said, "Naw, I don't want to go home. Just let me out." It had taken me this long to discover that he did not see well.

I went straight to his home. There, Mrs. Garcia said, "What ye want?" in the same belligerent tone that Pedro had used. The home consisted of one, overcrowded, filthy room with the father on a cot in a little lean-to room. Two dirty little girls were playing in a corner. They were using two rolled-up coats for

51

dolls. There was a smell of filth that I had not before encountered, and Mrs. Garcia was fat and greasy. And she smelled.

When I asked why Pedro did not come to school, she said that his father had been sick and Pedro had to help with the cows on the ranch. When the whiskey fumes from the lean-to became overpowering, she closed the door on her husband and opened the outside door for me.

The little girls walked to the door and smiled at me. They kept pushing their too-long, bushy hair out of their eyes. They were talking a little English. (They were all talking some English by October.)

As I left she said, "Don't turn Pedro in. He come back to school. He thirteen. The officer get him. Yes? Please?"

The little sisters, Lupe and Lucia, looked so much alike, so much like Pedro and so Indian. They were all stoic as Indians, so I was very glad to see the smiles.

Mrs. Burton had a clean, poorly furnished, two-room adobe house — sand color as always here. She had small, regular features and almost Negro black coloring. Mr. Burton looked pure Indian. They literally smothered Juanito with love. It was evident in their every loving glance and in Juanito's happy confidence.

Usually, Mexican parents smother their children with love, and the children thrive on it. Therein lies their security. Perhaps that is why it is so very difficult to get them to be away from the parents. After they learn the teacher can give them love, pull them onto her lap, and croon to ease the stumped toe or the loneliness for the mother, they return the same deep devotion. But the teacher must earn it. She has to prove that she loves them. It cannot be camouflaged. Children know if you love them, whether or not your crooning be in their native tongue. My children were beginning to know.

Juanito was tall and lanky and as fluid as water. He could not walk across the floor. He danced. All his parents wanted for him was an education. "Teasher, you teash him. He work, we see. He learn."

He did, and he loved school. He would use any contrived pretext to snuggle up to me, or look up at me and grin. He was thrilled with being alive. At this point he did not even know he was a Mexican, to say nothing of being part Negro. He had

52

learned security at home, and nothing had hurt him yet. Could he keep that? In all of Little Mexico, the Burton family constituted the only people the Garcias could look down upon because of the suspected Negro blood. Never in their lives would the Garcias rise to the level of the Burtons, morally or spiritually, but they did not know this. They felt superior because they were lighter in color. Two down and three to go. I wanted to meet all of them once and try, gradually, to get into their homes.

The clock said ten minutes after four when I went into the hotel lobby. Ophelia tore her eyes from the clock and walked up the stairs with me. She went to her room and I went to mine.

"Ah, 'scuse, teasher."

Mrs. Gonzales said she did not think I would be in so soon and she wanted to get a little cleaning done. She was digging in a corner with a toothbrush and cleanser — a corner that had never, in all the ages of the life of the Vidaurri, been touched. She said she would leave, and I asked her how Anna and Leandro were liking school.

She stopped her cleaning and began rolling her hands into her apron. She would roll the apron around them, then roll it back the other way, endlessly. A pleading tone came into her voice, and she said that the Mexican people would do anything I wanted if I would only stay. That the children liked school because I treated them nice and that they studied at home. They had never done that. Even Pedro, she said, brought his reading book home and went over the neighborhood helping the little ones with the hard English words, but that she thought he could not see very well.

She asked if she cleaned my room well enough. If I would just tell her how I wanted it done, she would do it. If I would leave my dirty hose and underclothing out, she would wash them. That she would love to do this. The Anglos, she said, did not know the Mexicans wanted a better life for the children. "Better than we have, but you — teasher — somehow, you know. Not only to learn English, but to learn good manners and keep the house and the children clean, and to be good in life and to fear God. To fear God," she repeated.

I told her I would not leave anything for her to wash and

53

that she took too much time with my room, but that I, too, wanted the same things for the children. However, I did tell her she could do something for me: every day she could leave a note in the contorted mirror; one Spanish word marked so I could pronounce it, and its English equivalent.

I did not know until much later how she went from door to door getting the words because she did not know how to write them.

"That is all? That is nothing. Yes, I do," she had said.

FIVE

school on Monday I took Pedro to the local doctor and had his
eyes fitted for glasses. He got the glasses right there. I had made
arrangements to pay for them, by the month, out of my check.
Pedro came in to school wearing the bright new glasses, with
the thick lens and the dark, cheap frames, smiling all over his
face. He sat down in his seat and began reading. I asked him to
read aloud and had the shock of my life.

"Sure, I read. I see now." After long, studied scrutiny he
said, "Teasher, you pretty."

He read, and he talked, and he sang, all in English. He was
able to read beyond first-grade level and picked up learning so
fast I could hardly believe it. He had a beautiful singing voice,
and I determined to ask Ophelia if she would give him voice
lessons. Ophelia could do anything, and it would be acceptable.
I think Ophelia could have done all the things I was trying to
do, with no comment from either race. When Pedro led the
group in singing "God Bless America," I couldn't join in. I was
choking.

I visited the Morin family next. Mrs. Morin was a tall blonde,
whether Castillian Spanish or a throw-back, or just part Anglo,
I did not know. She looked, acted, and spoke like an Anglo —
almost. She had a pre-glasses Pedro type of hatred for anything
as fair as she was. She said she sent the children to school to

55

learn . . . that they spoke English . . . that, yes, she was satisfied . . . and was there anything else?

I said that there was. Why did they not speak English at home, so the children would not have to learn it all at school?

She said she stopped speaking English long ago and that she was only doing it now because she knew I could not speak Spanish. This was not a token of respect to me, however. She told me I would be better off if I stuck with my own people. Her husband came in shyly, speaking a little English, and watching her for her approval, trying very hard to please her.

She looked at him as if she were thinking she would be an Anglo if she had not married a Mexican. Perhaps, she would. I did not know. Perhaps somewhere in the past, she had made a choice against the Anglo and was spending her married life regretting it — never letting her husband forget it. The little blue-eyed, dark-haired Nino and Paula seemed oblivious to any discord between their parents, but they seldom smiled.

By the first of November the children talked all the time. In fact, I sometimes had to stop them to get them to talk one at a time. They had lost much fear and tension. Praise and smiles did more to get them to work hard than I had thought possible with any children. They thrived on it. The little ones would trump up any excuse to get on my lap.

By the first of November we had, also, the bathroom. It had taken two months of planning and working. I never really thought it would do any good when I talked to Mrs. Gomez about it, and I did not hear anything until I came to school one morning, and they were working. In the end there were three little cubicles and a shower stall for both boys and girls.

After that I had the cleanest group of little ones anywhere. They would come to school with a rag and a little piece of soap, and by the time I arrived they would be waiting shining-clean and with satisfied grins on their faces. All day they would go to the little cublicles — to hear the water gush, I think. Many of them had never heard it.

One morning I went at fifteen minutes after seven to make lesson plans which I never did seem to be able to get done — and above the trickle of the water in the shower I heard Pedro singing "Ave Maria." I think I have never heard anything lovelier, and I am sure I will never hear anyone more suffused with the happiness of being alive.

Pedro said that he did not mean for me to hear him. That Miss Ophelia said to wait until it is perfect, then surprise the teacher. Would I not tell Miss Ophelia? If I did she might not teach him "Jesus Paid It All," and the preacher at the Baptist Mexican Mission in Holtville had promised Pedro he could sing it all by himself in church when he learned it.

No, I would not tell Miss Ophelia.

Pedro said that if he got to sing the song in church he would have to have a pair of shoes, and he wanted a new shirt and a new pair of jeans. Did I think Mr. Ortega would let him wash dishes in the cafe after school if he came to school early and took a bath every day?

I could have said, "Ask him," but it gave me an excuse to call Juan.

I knew many months later how we got the bathroom. Mrs. Gomez had had no success, so she had referred the problem to Juan. He tried to interest the fathers by offering to help them collect scrap pipe, old bathroom fixtures, and odd bits of wood and tin. He offered the services of his car. He offered to help them build it. He reminded them they could use money they spent for things they did not need, which they sometimes bought instead of the necessities of life. He explained what it would mean to the children in learning about cleanliness. He tried it all, he said, and finally, as they were walking away he said, "Miss Camish may leave if you don't put a bathroom onto that school."

This was a master stroke. In telling me about it he said, "I knew we could not run you off. I had already tried it. But, the fathers did not know that. They replied, "Why you so say teasher want? Sure we make. She want. We make. She stay. Eh?"

I can still picture him as he was the day they started the little cubicles: brown, in jeans with the brown hill behind him, standing on the ground in the October sun holding one end of the steel tape with one hand and a pencil and notebook in the other. I do not know who was on the other end of the tape. They both stood up. He said good morning.

Until then I only had one world — my classroom. Now, I

had two. My little ones laughing and learning and loving and just beyond the window I had Juan working for them — or for us. Or, was it for me? Whatever it was, his ritual never changed. Good morning was all he ever said while he worked on that job. All of October and part of November, he was outside my window a part of every day, but he never looked inside and never indicated in any other way that he was aware of my existence. But the little details I memorized for all time, as I would say to the children "Say after me . . . " I was impressing my memory with the Latin shrug which can mean many things, or nothing — anything they want it to express. The way he slowly walked around and surveyed the building project . . . the sunlight on the heavy-bluish hair . . . the rapid staccato Spanish . . . the slow deliberate movements and unhurried way of the Mexican . . . the turn of the head . . . the slow, sure movements of his hands . . . the voice . . . the voice . . .

Sometimes he would look toward the classroom but never inside. Were those slightly oriental eyes with the far-away look directed at the low-lying hills, misty, cloudy, and far away, seeing those hills or were they seeing nothing? Perhaps they were looking into a future too deep for sharing?

I liked the way he walked — tall, straight and unhurried. I liked the way he moved his hands slowly and gently. I liked his voice as the Spanish words came swiftly from his lips. Like all Latins? I don't know. To me, never.

The day the children copied the notes, the difficult combinations of symbols that in English invited the parents to come to see the bathrooms, was a highlight. Pedro brought a big box of candy and a box of cookies and a big pot of coffee. He said, "Miss Camish, I tell you a secret. Mr. Ortega, well, he send these things for the party, but you tell him he won't let me wash dishes no more. See?"

Payday, when I went to make a payment on Pedro's glasses, I was told, "They're paid for. Some Mexican. Don't know his name. All look alike. Names all sound alike, but this was a city-lookin' guy."

Why, Juan? Why? No matter what I try to do, you either stop it or make it easier. You refuse to have anything to do with me, and yet, in so many ways you take care of our needs. You

58

help me with so many big things, but in the one thing I want you are a block of solid, cold iron. Why?

They tell you everything, don't they? My Mexicans. Is it all only for your people? If so, why did you not do it before? All this and when I call your name you become a sheet of impenetrable ice. Tell me why?

Perry and Bob arrived at three o'clock on Saturday afternoon. When I came into the lobby Bob was saying to Ophelia, "I told you why I couldn't be here. I'll explain it all in detail later. Let's not talk about it now."

Ophelia had on a bright green chiffon dress with long sleeves and ruffles at the throat and the always matching shoes and no jewelry. Her eyes looked bright green and unhappy. She suggested we all drive to Holtville.

I put on my red dress and my red shoes and wore my red beads which constituted the only outfit of clothing I owned that was all the same color.

The road was dry, dry dirt and twisty — twisting around through the low hills in the glaring sun. We drove fast which only made the wind hotter.

You don't arrive in Holtville. You come over a low hill, and there it is, lying in a little valley, sunning itself among the old, weather-beaten rocks and dry vegetation. You could drive into Holtville every day of your life, and if you were not thinking about it, you would be surprised when the village loomed up, in front of you.

"Nothing in Holtville. Let's go right on across the river," Bob said.

Ophelia beamed like a well-fed baby.

Well, what would we come here for but to cross the river? Did one come to Holtville with any other pre-ordained conclusion than going across the river? Otherwise, one would stop on the American side.

"After Chaparral you call this a city," Bob said. "But this is no city. There are . . . let's see . . . maybe twenty, thirty thousand people here, most of them Mexican. No, I wouldn't call that a town, almost no white people. But, across the river, now, there are about ten thousand people . . . Mexicans, that is. No whites

59

live on the other side . . . oh, maybe a few poor white trash married to Mexicans."

Bob had the same black and white attitude toward the nationalities that most of the Vidaurri citizens and most of Chaparral had.

The river was low, muddy, sort of reddish-brown. It was not too wide, and it disappointed me only because I had not known what to expect. It did not have much water. But it was a big river, really a big river. There was nothing like it where I came from.

Perry said, "You call this a river. People in this part of the country don't know what a river is. Why up north, they wouldn't even call this a creek."

I did not like it. "To me, this is a river. It is *the* river. It's the biggest river I ever saw, and I don't care what's up north. This is a Texas river."

"Well, Hon! I just mean there are real rivers. I don't care what they have up north either. But I'd question whether this is a Texas river or a Mexican river."

Bob said, "To tell the truth, nobody knows. They don't even know who the land belongs to; I mean whether it's Texas or Mexico. This river used to go right along there," he said, pointing vaguely toward a space of dry land on the American side. "Ever since the river changed course, the two governments have been arguing about who it belongs to. Every few years the river changes again, and the wrangle starts all over. Nobody ever wins. The Mexicans make their claim; the Americans make their claim, and nothing happens. The line stays where the river runs now, not at the place it ran some time in the past."

"They could have a flood again, and it would change again then. This river is not a permanent thing, is it? The river is not as mixed up as some of us are?" I asked.

Perry said, "Hon, you feel all right? We're just talking about how the river has changed its course. I guess there could be another big flood; there could be a twelve-inch snowfall in *Monterrey,* too, but nobody would believe it."

I mused about "The Silvery Rio Grande." I was actually crossing it, but it did not look like the things I had heard about it.

60

"In one way you might be right," Perry said. "This is not considered a big river by measurement, but in changing a whole way of life; you're in a different world. This could be the widest river you'll ever cross."

I wondered again if he were referring to my episode across the little ditch into Little Mexico, and if he knew that I wanted to cross this river for always.

"Yeah," he said, "no matter how far you go, or what rivers you cross, this is probably the widest. Even after crossing the International Peace Bridge into Canada, you are still with your own kind of people."

I was not impressed. I was, just now for the first time, getting out of Texas.

Perry said, "Yes, right here, right about here, a whole new set of customs and ideals and ideas take over."

I knew we were on the Mexican side. Without thinking, my words spilled out. "You mean the split-second our car tires hit the Mexican dirt, or do the new set of customs take over in the exact middle of the river, or could it sometimes go a little way onto either side? Could each side ever spill over and get just a little intermingled?"

Ophelia was silent. She moved around as though she did not enjoy the conversation. Bob looked at her. Perry looked at me, and I saw disgust in his eyes. "That must be the school teacher taking over. But, do me something, Hon, will you? Just be quiet and listen, and maybe you'll learn something some time."

I pictured myself standing in the exact center of the river, holding out both hands, wide, one to the Mexican side and one to the American side. If we all caught hands . . . why couldn't we? Why this dark, straight line that could not be broken? Why could it not be budged one fraction?

The Old Town was lovely — and Mexican. It looked no more like Chaparral or Little Mexico than Chaparral looked like Dallas. And Dallas looks like nothing else. Even in Texas, Dallas looks like no other place. The Old Town had narrow streets lined with shops where merchandise spilled out over little bars and shelves onto the narrow walks. In this particular section, the tourist section, there were places for eating, drinking and shopping. The smells of frying foods — tortillas, baking enchila-

61

das, mixings for guacamole — made me hungry. A couple of drinks made Perry and Bob hungry to eat enough for four people. Perry bought me a pair of green beads and a bracelet.

"That's what the Mexicans wear. You want that stuff? Wear it to school. Oh, I don't care, Hon. Wear it with me if you like the stuff. Some day, I'll get you some good jewelry."

"You seem to like their food, their drinks, their music and their dancing. O.K., I like the jewelry, too."

"Hon, let's hush. What are we fighting about?"

Mexican places . . . night places . . . dark, mysterious entrances leave you with eager anticipation for the romantic mystery that must be inside if you are young and still impressionable. Someone meets you at the door, checks you quietly, courteously and secretly, so that by the time you are really in you have really accomplished something! Years later, you discover that they all use this same approach; anybody with the right clothes and the right amount of money can get into any nightclub in the world. Some times I am sorry to know this. The thrill and the wonder and the mystery of that night have long vanished. It was only a cheap dive, even though it was the best Holtville had to offer, but for me it was wonderful and suffused with mystery and drama.

The floor show was colorful in many ways. I did not understand all the jokes — then, I didn't. I laughed at all the wrong times. I understood the Mexican music without knowing why and without being able to explain its meaning. I felt it. We danced to Mexican music, and it was as if I had always known how to dance this way. It was a rhythmic thing that got into my feet and into my body and gave a throbbing life to all of me. My emotions took over, and I automatically put it into the dance. No wonder the Mexicans loved to dance and did it with such grace and ease.

Perry said, "You're a natural, Hon." And, I was so preoccupied with myself that I did not realize that he had said something nice to me. For me, he was not there anyway. I was alone. It was something over which I had no control. Something in the music and the night and in the haunting, romantic Mexican rhythm that did all this to me. I could not explain this to Perry. He had no imagination, none at all. He was practical and at

62

times critical to the point of being dull, but I thought he was a man of the world. I did not know how to impress him, so I did not try. There was nothing important to me but this dance, and I could not share that with Perry. I think Juan would have understood, but I would never know. Juan had placed himself out of my world.

Oh, yes. There was something — an indefinable thing, a new thing — a kind of bewildered yearning. The same queer longing I had felt when I put my hand in Juan's hair. It was an elusive thing, a thing so vague I could never define it, but a very real, completely alive thing and I relived it as we ate and danced. Perry was quiet, and I was grateful to feel this secondtime mood without interruption.

Finally, Perry said, "Look at the couple dancing. Now, look at the couples at the tables. Look at the couples at the bar."

I did. Well . . .

He said, "They're all in the same building, and that is the only thing you can say that is any ways near alike about them. Mexicans with Mexicans and Americans with Americans. Do you see any mixed couples? Each group is completely unaware that another country's citizens are on the same dance floor. Do you think any of them are worried about the other race, Hon? Do you think any one of them would go to bat for the other? Do you think there is one Mexican here who would sacrifice one dime for you?"

I felt indignant. "I don't know why you should even think of such a thing to talk about," I said. "You're always telling me to 'leave it alone' and 'let's have a good time,' so suppose we do. You're not the type to go to a night club to discuss race problems. You go for fun wherever you go."

"Think a minute, will you Jennie? Do you think they would stick their necks out for you? I'll bet you my next pay check that not one Mexican on that dance floor would lift a finger if I started to beat up on you."

"On that, you are right, of course. They wouldn't. In the Mexican code of behaviour, I am your woman, what you do to me, or with me, is your business. I know that much about them, Perry. You belong to one, you are his, but I am not yours, see?"

"I'm doing a pretty poor job on this," he said.

"I also agree with you on that. I'm not interested in your attempted analogy."

In fact, I did wish he would shut up. I did not know whether he was talking about my trying to get better things for my children and their parents, or whether he was talking about my . . . I almost said "my Juan."

"Hon, now you've just got to see that you can't fight a race battle. That's for big cities, with clubs and crazy organizations. That's for people who want to get their names in the paper, people who think it's smart to play like they're fighting for a cause. If you read the news, you will see that all they create is trouble. They never win."

I looked toward the dance floor. I was bored with Perry. He could have done a better job of whatever he was trying to do if we had been parked in the dip. The colors flashing by weren't conducive to serious thinking on my part. Perry fitted in the dip and in the Vidaurri and in Lee's. He did not fit here.

"The role you're playing is not for you, Hon. There's nothing tough about you. That's the type that goes in for race fights. You'd better stick with the Vidaurri crowd. Straighten yourself out and straighten Hilda out. Just go around with her and Ophelia, and you won't get into any trouble."

Ophelia and Bob had not missed a dance; yet they had hardly danced. They moved slowly and languidly along the floor. They barely moved. They were a marvelous couple when dancing. They were a bit of perfection. Now, they were two handsome people, talking, talking constantly, alone on a crowded dance floor. This I saw as I half-listened to Perry. I hoped Perry had had his say.

I said mine. "You are telling me to stick with the Vidaurri. Do you know who they are? Bert is forever, in his dignified manner, running the Mexicans down. He can say more with the lift of an eyebrow than most people can with a lecture. Lou meekly looks agreement, like a puppet, every time the eyelash flickers if it's her Bert. Falop and Lee have their happiest moments running down the Mexicans with volubility, and they haven't the remotest idea what they're talking about. Chaparral and the Vidaurri are filled with little people who never look below the surface at the person. And, Perry, I'm sorry but you sound like

64

one of them . . . the people who label the Mexicans only because they are not Anglos. Only Hilda will agree with me. Whatever Ophelia thinks, she keeps her mouth shut. I've never heard Ophelia say an unkind word about any person, regardless of race. Now, they, too, are part of the Vidaurri crowd. You tell me to stick with this crowd. They are not all the same. What kind of people? I'm afraid I will have to do my own choosing. I'd like to trade a few of the deceitful lot in on one good Mexican. Now, you know how I feel, and I don't think you are going to be able to change it."

I was glad, immediately glad that Ophelia and Bob came back to the table about that time. Perry looked as though I had given him quite a blow — I who had only listened thus far. Ophelia looked as though she had been crying. Bob immediately began letting go with his particular brand of charm, which I admit was a load of charm. He looked as though nothing had happened to him. Everything was fine — just fine with everybody. Ophelia looked as though she had been through the valley of death — alone. It was the first time I had seen her charming composure fail her. We exchanged dances, and then danced one more time.

Back at our table Perry tried the salty-dog approach again. "Just a sip, Hon. It will make you feel better. You're all upset. I didn't mean to upset you."

"I certainly am upset, and I don't want a salty-dog, now or ever. I don't like them. You do the drinking."

As of one accord, without discussion, we started home. As we walked out the door, we met them coming in — Juan and the girl he had been with the night of the dance palace tragedy. Juan looked furious and as though he had been standing there for some time. I guess he had.

The waiter said, "Would you like to go in now, Mr. Ortega?"

Juan looked at me; I looked at him. Neither of us spoke. But we looked long and searchingly. He was the first to move away. Perry looked at me, and I felt that he knew. Somehow, he knew about that night. Being Perry, why didn't he give me a lecture on it? He lectured all around it. Was he trying to get me to "confess"? It was a short, quiet ride home. Perry looked straight ahead and drove fast, as if he felt his life depended on speed.

Who would tell Perry? In Tulsa, how could he know? People in Chaparral did not even know how I sprained my ankle. Or did they?

Before we reached the Vidaurri I asked, "Why did you call me to tell me to stay in my room and keep Hilda with me, as if I didn't have the intelligence to walk down the street alone?"

He said, "I think I've already said it all. But I'll add on if you like because you'd probably walk in the wrong direction. You think entirely too much of the Mexicans, Hon, and it's dangerous. You're going to get into serious trouble some time. You talk too much. You can't change the whole world, you know. Some Mexican might just knife you in the back. I know Mexicans. Have known them all my life. You can't trust them. You need somebody here to protect you. I worry about you, and I can't stay here, so I called."

I did not trust myself to comment. My fury would surely have been too evident.

There was something about being back — each time we left for even short periods of time — back at the Vidaurri, a feeling of security. I had been living there almost three months and I felt, when I would return, "I'm home." I liked Perry better here; he belonged. The minute we walked into the lobby, we all came back to life. It was as if we had been waiting for this, for this coming home. You could hear the three-piece orchestra from Lee's two blocks away. Perhaps, because on Saturday nights, you were always listening for it. The girl from Holtville was singing:

"Alla en el Rancho Grande,
Alla donde vivia . . . "

and, as always, I wanted to say "ya-ha" and dance. The girl was a redhead, but she had not always been. She had only a fair singing voice, but the lovely Spanish words made it musical. The couples were dancing the stomping Vidaurri style, and the thought came to me: So many Anglos, so often, run down the Mexicans for "facts" about which they know nothing. I want to ya-ha and stomp only when the Mexican music says so. What

66

a lovely dance is the proper Mexican dance to "Rancho Grande." I had seen the Anglos dance to the jarabe, a long involved, many-parts dance done step-by-step just as the music says. One of the most beautiful dances as far south as you can go across our border. The Anglos literally ruined it. So few of them ever tried even the basic step, which is unlike any step we have in an American dance. They would do a two-step and a little jitterbug, with always the off-time stomping in the wrong places. The orchestra would play a cowboy tune next, and they would do the same things to the different music.

Some of the time we would sing in Spanish as we danced. We thought we were singing in Spanish; I learned later we were ruining that, too.

We ate the food, gulping it down and complaining about the grease and the heat in it. Authentic Mexican food, carefully prepared. We ruined it with lack of appreciation.

I had heard the Anglos loud and long. It came to me what justifiable criticisms must take place in Little Mexico regarding the rude gringos. I think that night I really began to drift to the other side. Until then I may have had Juan mixed up with the children and did not always know what I was talking about. I knew I was always thinking about Juan, regardless of what else might be on my mind or what I might be doing.

I realized that we could say anything we wanted to about or to a Mexican. They could only say things about us. With sudden insight I knew what Hilda meant by being a member of a minority race, and I realized her family must have suffered in a similar fashion.

"Want to dance, Hon?" Asked Perry.

"No, let's go get some coffee."

Lee was talking to some couple who had just come in. "I wish you'd just go upstairs and listen to that Mexican girl jabbering away in Spanish. No voice at all and the silly Mexican words. The boys in the orchestra look as if they'd like to love her to pieces. Beats me. I'll get a white orchestra here if the guy who owns the place ever comes to town, or if I could even find him by phone."

"But we don't want a white orchestra."

"Sure, Lee, it's not music, but it's different."

"You're making money; guess that's the main thing."

"We get kind of a kick out of those boys, Lee."

They loved the Mexican music and the orchestra so much, they intended to keep it; but they wouldn't admit it.

Falop said, "Well, you all been havin' a cup of coffee, huh?" He was being very cordial to the oil boys tonight. "Got somethin' a little stronger out here in the car."

We thanked him and he wandered on to another table — the big business man exuding good will.

Perry said, "Jennie, he's got the right idea, especially for Saturday night. We should have had a drink with him. He's a good fellow. You notice he didn't say a word about Ophelia not being at the store tonight."

Ophelia said, "It didn't matter. The clothes sell themselves. I recognize them." Then she told us the cost of every dress in the cafe and that the dresses had been hanging on the racks when she left the store at two o'clock. She had called Falop to come to the store so she could go with us. I guess he had made so much money that night that he felt he could afford to be generous with Ophelia and with his bottle.

Perry said to Lee, "You know this girl barely knows the taste of a salty dog? On a hot night by the fan or a cold night by the fire, this girl doesn't know how good a salty dog is."

Lee said, "She don't know what she's missin'," as if I were missing my quinine. I thought she must not really like them either.

Perry said, "Hon, let me mix you one." He mixed four. Ophelia did not touch hers. She did not even move it out of her way; she just reached over it for her coffee as if she did not know it was there. I think she really did not see it that night.

"Just drink it down, Hon. Give you a lift," Perry said, just as the Mexican orchestra passed behind us. I sipped it. It tasted salty and bitter.

The oil boy who had lost all his money in the poker game the last time was winning. He had a look of deep concentration on his face. This was a business deal to him. He did not have money to throw away, and he would try to get a little of his money back tonight, if he could.

The ranchers were keeping the bids down so he could stay

68

with them. Did they intend to let him win? Were they really not cruel, but just accustomed to big money? Hank was being very polite to him, and I wondered if the previous time had been only because he was angry with Ophelia. No, she was standing there tonight with Bob, watching them play, and Hank spoke civilly.

Bob said, "Let's go," and Perry said, "You go on with Ophelia and Bob, Hon." Aside to me he said, "Never know what will happen here before morning. I better stick around. You get some sleep, Hon. I'll stay here with Bunk."

So, that was his name.

SIX

OPHELIA
and Bob left me at the lobby door and drove off in his car. I
went on up to get some sleep, but I was not sleepy. I came down
to sit on the veranda, and there were couples sitting around everywhere. There was not an inch of private space. I went just to
the end of the veranda at the corner and behind the hotel and
sat in Cava's old "Rheumatism Chair" where he sat to rest
when he ached in his joints, as he said. I watched the pale moon
over the little hill. It was a dark, cool, November night, with
just a little chill in the air. I felt it through my sweater.

For the first time, Perry bored me tonight. Really bored me.
Usually it has been fun just being anywhere if Ophelia is there
. . . I'll have to keep seeing him — that is if he wants to see me
after the way I talked to him tonight ...Hilda says it is the only
thing to do . . . even though the murder has stopped being front-
page news, it will crop up again. Just last week there was a
note saying that the police knew who the fellow was and that
if he would give himself up, they would be easier on him. I can
see through this ruse . . . my intelligent Mexicans can too. The
Anglos have underrated the Mexicans for so many years, they
do not know how to stop. How odd it would be if they discovered that an Anglo had fired that shot! What would they do
then? Soft-pedal the punishment? or just nothing at all?

There was never any background on the boy who was shot.
He lived in Old Mexico and had only driven through Chaparral,

70

but the lights at the dance palace had attracted him. His body and personal effects had been sent to some little place in Mexico, along with his car, and that was all that anybody knew . . . Nobody knew him in Little Mexico . . . The police had no motive, no clues and nobody to accuse. They were really playing it by ear, and they would play it that way until they decided to pin it on somebody . . . Mexican, of course.

Why was I bored with Perry? He was no different. He was a dictator to me, a fact which had bothered me none until tonight. Before, I just listened and did as I chose. Was it because I wanted Juan so much that I was dissatisfied with everybody else? Did I really want Juan, or just want to know that I could have him? I thought I wanted the man, himself, but I would have to go out with Perry and go along with the crowd until the murder was settled, whatever was decided to do . . . I would go, but eventually . . .

Then, I heard Bob's voice just around the corner. It came from the section that had the big, comfortable wicker chairs.

"I *couldn't* leave. I know it's the longest I've stayed away since I met you, but I couldn't leave. I called you every time I could. I missed you, baby."

Ophelia answered, "I know clothes, Bob. I could work in a dress shop anywhere in the world. In a city I would have a better opportunity. I would like to be a buyer, and I believe that I've had enough experience to do it and make a lot more money than I make here."

"Baby, don't." I could imagine Bob's head buried in his hands. His voice sounded muffled and hurt. "Please, baby, we've been over all of that."

"We could manage," Ophelia said.

"Yes," he said, "we could manage. Year after year you would think less and less of me until we just fell apart. I couldn't take it, knowing I could do nothing for you, knowing it couldn't last."

"It would work out all right, Bob," Ophelia said.

"No," Bob replied.

I knew I should go inside but I could not move. Cava's old chair had only one rocker and it made terrible noises if you moved — even a little move. I was hot and then cold and my throat ached for Ophelia.

"Come here, baby," Bob said, "and I'll cue you in one more time."

Ophelia was crying softly, so softly I thought at first that I was mistaken. It was a tiny, kitten sort of wail — faint and protesting, as if she had heard Bob's story many times; but he started it again.

"Mostly, I'm a pretty sorry guy, but this one thing I cannot do. Don't you see that I could never let her down? I'm all she has. Sure, I have a good job, but not good enough to take care of you, too. You must see that, baby? Right now it's rough."

Through her muffled sobs Ophelia said, "But I wouldn't cost you anything."

"I wouldn't have a wife who wouldn't cost me anything. I wouldn't be able to take it that way." I heard him stand up and start toward her. "Do something for me, baby. Leave it alone for now, huh?"

I eased out of Cava's old chair and ran.

I felt sick and ashamed. I knew Ophelia would never have been so curious or disloyal as I had been. She would not have eavesdropped when my heart was unburdening itself. I could not even talk to Hilda about this. I hurt all over, for my own guilt. I hated Bob for not wanting to marry her, and I hated myself for knowing it. Most of the single men in the county would love to be married to Ophelia. Even the wives loved her. I guess almost everyone loved Ophelia. I did not know I could so quickly despise somebody over a conversation I did not understand.

It was obvious that Bob was married. Had he not said that he "couldn't let her down"? How could Ophelia love this man who was married? How could she tolerate this conversation with him? How could he stand himself?

About eleven o'clock Hilda came in. Between listening to Ophelia's slow, tortured movements in her room, Hilda told me she had been with Toolie, that Toolie had refused to talk for about a month. She would talk to Hilda today, but she had not for the past three weeks. She said she had not talked because she had decided to kill her brother. This decision had taken her a while to make, but now she knew. She would use a gun. He had missed two whole weeks of coming to see her, and she thought she would feel better after she killed him. No, her husband had not been to see her in months, she had said, but she would think about him when she got rid of her brother. Oh, she said, it was her husband she was going to kill. She forgot; her brother did come to see her.

She let Hilda wash her long, blonde hair which was filthy. She had smiled dreamily and said, "Now, that we have made our plans, I can go to sleep. I'll let you know when I need you again. Thank you for coming."

I went to bed and tried to think up excuses for staying to hear Ophelia and Bob talk. I knew they heard me leave, the old rocker did make a noise; they must have seen me. All the rationalizing did no good. I could not forgive myself. It was just one more conversation I could not discuss with Hilda. This I could tell no one. I lay awake most of the night and around morning I decided I had to tell Ophelia that I had overheard.

We could hear Lee and Bunk arguing down in the lobby the next morning.

"Yes," Bunk was saying, "I got my money back and a little extra, and I'll buy you anything you want to eat. I'll take you anywhere you want to go. But, I will *not* buy you any gin. I know about that stuff. I tried it. You've had too much already. Now, do you want to ride around in the car or go up to bed?"

Cava said, "Miss Lee, the guests, they all asleep. Miss Lee, you betta git quieta. Mr. Bunk, you tell her."

Bunk was making a lot of noise, but he was not drinking. "I don't want to ride around. I don't want to eat. I don't want to sleep. I just want a drink, you cheap skate."

"You're already full up to here," Lee made a leveling motion across her throat.

"You go ahead, Lee. Say anything you want to. You know I can't get gin at this hour."

"I know it. You've got some in your car, though."

"Yes, I have, Lee. It's not mine, but it's there, and there it will stay. It belongs to Perry. He didn't want it in his car — said his girl might think he was drinking too much. Said she sort of told him off tonight, so he left the gin in my car."

How little his girl thought. I did not know whether he drank a little, a lot, or enough. He acted the same way every time I saw him.

I went to see Ophelia. She looked hurt. It was deep in her eyes and in the far reaches of her mind. The hurt was showing, deep and cruel. I realized that she had had a worse night than I. When I told her that I had listened to her and Bob as they talked on the veranda she looked even more tired and desolate, but not angry. Just hopeless.

"Don't worry about me, Jennie. Everything is going to be all right. One way or the other, it has to be."

She looked so little and pretty and helpless that I hated Bob more than ever. He was doing something to her that made her look like this, feel like this, act like this. And, it was wrong. Essentially Ophelia was a happy person.

She said, "Hilda slept and wrote to Carl all weekend. It was the longest letter, Jennie. I don't know what in the world she could find to write so many pages about." And, she smiled a sad, tired smile.

"She's in love with him. Don't you know that, Ophelia?"

"No, not twenty pages worth, I don't know. And, the guy in South America."

"Love makes anything possible and seems to make reason out of unreason, I guess." I knew the conversation made little sense, but I had to say something because she wanted talk. She wanted to talk in order to skirt around her conversation with Bob.

She said, "A lot of words are said trying to make love, to be loved and to give love — when there's no love there. It's even worse when that love is not possible to be fulfilled."

I hope she would go on, but that was to be her contribution to our conversation.

I said, "Have you seen Perry?"

She said he was having coffee in Lee's, and had asked her why she did not go home. He hadn't meant back to the Vidaurri. He had meant to wherever she came from.

"I don't want to go home. I don't ever want to go home. Wherever that might be. I've only known Chaparral, as a home, I mean. I want to stay right here."

I told her, "Perry has the solution to everybody's problems, except his own. He's tried to send me home several times, yet he wants me around when he decides to drop in. Perry is not without problems. I don't know what they are, but he's so busy drinking and trying to have fun that he loses the whole point of life. He hasn't time to relax and enjoy it. I don't pay any attention to him. I want to stay here, too, and I intend to regardless of the people who would like to see me leave."

She said, "I agree with all of it, except, Jennie, they have to 'drop in.' They can't do it any other way. That, they can't help."

In any case I knew I did not want to go home, ever. I was at home. I was in Chaparral.

After church, Cava gave me the Little Mexico telephone number to call. Mrs. Gomez asked me to come by her house after school the next day, or asked if she might come to the school. I did not want to see Perry, so I asked, "May I come right now?"

Mrs. Gomez had three clean, fresh-smelling adobe rooms. She had hot Mexican sweet bread just coming out of the oven and a pot of fresh coffee. She was embarrassed so I started talking about the children. She said they all spoke English at home now, and all they wanted was a good life for their children — better than they had. She tried to express her appreciation for my efforts and then she said her husband had told her she must talk to me.

The men were beginning to plan how the dance palace could be re-built. They were there on the side of the hill, now. Mr. Ortega said new holes should be dug for the poles to hold it up, that the poles should be pipes buried deep in the ground so that never again should it be allowed to fall.

"My husband said, but he was teasing, Miss Camish. He meant no harm, and no lack of respect. He was teasing, please believe."

I wondered for many minutes what her husband had said, as she wrung her hands and tried to think how to go on.

Finally, she repeated his words: "Yes, we will build it right. Some white girl might get hurt here," and she laughed. "You see, he was really only teasing, Miss Camish."

"I know Mr. Ortega took you to his home," she continued. "I saw the doctor's car. My husband only heard that you and Miss Smaltz were at the dance, so he didn't know."

"That's all right, Mrs. Gomez," I said.

"There is more," she said. "Mr. Ortega hit my husband, oh, many times. His eyes are closed and his face is black. I think Mr. Ortega kill him if the men didn't stop him. My husband looks awful, but he will be all right.

"I'm so sorry, Mrs. Gomez. I — "

"Oh, that's nothing," she interrupted. "He apologize to Mr. Ortega and I apologize to you. We — the Mexican people, would never say anything against you or Mr. Ortega. Both of you we like, we respect. Mr. Ortega say he kill a man talk about you."

I think we were both highly embarrassed.

She said, "We want you to like us. You help our children. We want you to stay here with us. If I say too much, forgive me." Then she added, "I must say this. My husband did not tell me to say this, but I know. We know how Mr. Ortega feel about you. It is sad. Love is hard even if both of same race. We grieve for him. If ever anything I can do, you tell me. My house is your house. Please go now."

Many times I had gone over bits and pieces of the night in Juan's apartment. I had tried to kill the memories each time by staying too busy to think. Sunday night I went to bed to go over it all again — I thought . . . I had put my fingers in his hair . . . He had jumped back and stared at me as if he thought I was crazy . . . He had said, "Don't do that. You don't know what you're doing."

"I'm doing exactly what I want to do."

"You're so blonde and so beautiful," he had said, still standing there — across the room.

Now the only criterion by which I could be judged blonde was by process of elimination — I was not a brunette. The only criterion by which I could be called beautiful was youth. I had never — until that night — been called either blonde or beautiful.

The longer he had stayed away from me the more I wanted to have him close to me. I had started toward him, but my sprained ankle had not held up. I fell half-way across the room. I am tall. He picked me up, wrapped a blanket around me, and placed me in the big chair by the window. He propped my foot on pillows, then sat in a straight chair facing me, near but not near enough for me to touch him. He looked out the window and he started talking.

"Who are you, Jennie? Who are your people? Why did you come here?"

I told him about the aunt who had died and that I had, at first, wanted to come here only because of the money. I told him I came from a little place called Musgrove. No, he had never heard of it.

"Please, tell me about you," I said.

He seemed to want to do this. Then, perhaps, I would understand and maybe, leave him alone.

"When I was a little boy in Old Mexico I wanted to come to America. That's all I wanted. I don't know why now. I had everything I needed there. My family had not much money, but enough. They had enough influence and enough friends in the town, and we were happy enough. I finished high school there, and still I wanted to come to America. I wanted to go to an American university. I didn't want, at that time, an American girl. I'd never thought of the kind of girl I wanted. My mother was strongly opposed to my crossing the river. My dad thought that was the road to progress — that it led across the river. But my grandmother — she was the one, the one who really encouraged me. All my life I went to her with my problems, big ones, little ones, and she had an answer for them all. The strange thing was that she knew, better than my mother, the hurt and humiliation I might run into. My mother hasn't yet crossed the river, and she never will. In our town there were several Mexican-American couples. I didn't know the differences until I grew up, and then only vaguely. They were well-thought of, had nice families. The Mexicans and the Americans lived together in that town, in harmony. I thought they did anywhere. The children grew up feeling that there was no difference. Of course, some of them crossed the river and never came home again after they grew up. They had to choose, but I still wasn't making any choice. I'm not ready to, yet. Even though my mother kept trying to explain to me that life would be different across the river, it was just words."

77

He looked at me for the first time. "Tell me if you're bored. Are you comfortable? It seems I have to tell you these things. Then, perhaps you'll understand."

"Yes, I mean, no. Go on."

"I knew what I wanted, in the way of education, when I went to college. My dad had a hotel at home and that was what I wanted, hotel management. Everything went fine for two years. I met a girl. I'd gone with her for those two years. Then, her parents came to see her. Up until then I'd been accepted just as I had at home. It wasn't anything the parents said or did, or anything they said to her. It was an attitude of looking down. I could feel them looking down, like I do when I walk down the street in Chaparral. It wasn't an open bitterness as it is here, but it was there, unmistakenly there. She felt it, too. After her parents left, we just drifted apart."

He was still looking out the window, at the blue-black hills and the scattered dim lights.

"Oh, Jennie, Jennie. Why am I telling you all this? It's a cruel thing for me to want an American girl. It's more cruel to want to marry one. For me, it would never work. It would never work because *I* know it wouldn't. You see, Jennie, the Mexican has to make the decision on this side of the river. The American has no decision to make. His life is already arranged. When we cross the river, we make the first decision. Now I know how lucky and how really smart the ones who stayed home are. I used to think they didn't have any ambition. They were the ones who did the intelligent thing. How can you know when you're right, Jennie? For an American girl, I would always be afraid of embarrassment for her — for me, and to think, I just had to cross a river — and not one of the big ones — to find out."

Looking at me he added, "I got over that girl — well over her, long ago, but that's where I learned." A far-away, thoughtful look grew in Juan's eyes. "I got over her, but I learned about the thing my mother had feared for me, though why she should be so bitter against my crossing the river, I don't understand yet. I know why, but I don't understand it."

"Why? Juan, tell me why."

"You wouldn't understand either. After the four years in college I was completely lost. A college education was the worst thing that could possibly have happened to me. I didn't want to go home. I didn't want to stay there. I wandered around for awhile. How old are you, Jennie?"

"I'm twenty-one — soon I will be."

"I thought so. I'm thirty-one. I've been a lot more places than you have. I know many things about life that you don't know. You don't see the problems at all. No other American girl in Chaparral would be here."

"Hilda would — if she loved a man, she would."

"You don't know anything about love, Jennie. You know only that the forbidden feels like love, and it may not be love at all. Why did you come here, Jennie? Why did you want to come over here?"

"I don't know now. What did you do next?"

"I had some money from my father. I wanted to get lost in a small town. This one is small enough! There was an opening for a cafe here. It seemed like a good place to stop."

"How did you know about the place?"

He laughed a little and said, "Don't ever answer an ad in the paper. These people had no decent place to eat, and they wanted a cafe. It's the kind of work I know and like, and I'm doing all right here."

"I love this apartment," I said. And, he just looked at me, looked at me for a long, long time. Then he spoke again.

"You — and Hilda — you would love any place where you would be happy. You don't know yet what that would be. I couldn't compete with the ranchers, but I could with the oil boys," and he laughed a flat laugh. "That's really all, Jennie. You're young. Nothing has hurt you yet, and I don't intend to help it along." Before I could comment, he continued, "Do you go to church, Jennie?"

"Sure," I said, "I'm a Baptist. I go to church every Sunday. Well, most every Sunday." I didn't go when Perry was in town. "Are you Catholic?"

"No, Jennie. That is an Anglo misconception. Not all Mexicans are Catholics. The largest Mexican church in Holtville is Baptist. I go there. There are only three families of Mexican Baptists here, and we couldn't get a preacher. Mrs. Morin won't go anywhere, and Mrs. Garcia says she doesn't like to dress up.

79

The other three are from your classroom. You should see us Jennie. The Gomez family has a car, and mine. We look like the Jodes going to California."

Juan's Buick was a red club coupê. He said most of the time he didn't even need the one extra seat. When I asked him about Sunday school he looked sort of sheepish and said, "I teach the same little ones that you have in school, plus some from Holtville. I don't feel qualified, but Brother Luz insists that I am, so I try. I read the Bible, and he helps me. I teach them the same things that you do: to fear the Lord and — well, just what the Bible says, I try, I mean. It is so hard to get across."

I said, "I know how hard it is to get across. You can know what you want to teach, but getting it across is something else."

"I often think it must be very hard to try to teach all week what I try only on Sunday."

I kept trying to bring him back to me. "I wish you could go to church with me, or I with you."

He sighed. "Go ahead and wish I were Anglo. Might as well make the wish a good one since none of it can ever happen anyway. I know, Jennie, my bitterness is showing."

"I don't want you to be Anglo. I just want you to be what you are."

"I haven't always been what I am. That is why I try so hard. Jennie, I have a lot of bad living in my past to live down. That is what I want to do."

"You couldn't have been very bad."

"You wouldn't believe it if I told you, but I don't intend to tell you, so it's all right. You just continue to think well of me. That is all. Just as a friend."

"Why don't you like me?" I asked. I knew this was a stupid question, but I wanted him to say something. He did. He could have said it to anybody.

"I didn't say that, Jennie. I do like you. That's all I want, just to like you; there's nothing but pain any other way. I know. I've seen it in my mother, in my own family. My mother was a result of a love that should never have been."

"Are you sure of that? How do you know the happiness she may have had also?"

"I see. I don't really know." He glanced at the clock and

then, in a shocked tone, he said, "It's almost three o'clock. I must get you home. I'll wake Miss Smaltz."

"No, Juan, please not yet."

He stood over me with his slanty black eyes boring into mine and very definitely told me what our relationship would be.

"I'll never recognize you on the streets. I'll never see you in a crowd. If I have to speak to you I will say, 'Miss Camish.' That is all. You must act as if this night never happened; act the same way. You don't know me. You never saw me in your life. We can't even be friends in public, and Jennie, I don't want a hidden affair regardless of how innocent it might be. Nobody would believe the innocence; only we would know, and that, my little one, will never get you far in this world. Jennie, promise me that you will never cross that line again, except to go to work. Do not come again at night."

"I cannot promise that. That is impossible. I want to see you."

"It isn't impossible unless you want a lot of trouble. You have a good reputation, and you'll lose it Jennie if Chaparral ever discovers you have been to Little Mexico, unescorted, after school hours. What do you think they would say if they knew you had spent most of the night in this apartment? Jennie you could tell them we talked all night; you could tell them that to the end of your days, and I promise you not one of them would ever believe it."

"What about the Mexican people?"

"I don't know. If you were a Mexican girl, my girl here, it would be all right. But an Anglo, I don't know what they would think. You see if you can figure out what they would think."

"I don't care."

"Not tonight, you don't. But you'll have a long time to remember tonight, Jennie, if we don't stop the story before it starts."

"Juan. Please, sit down again."

SEVEN

HILDA
came rushing into my room and switched on the light and
brought me back to this world. I didn't like it; I liked the other
one better.

"I had to be Holtville all day," she said. "Toolie is worse.
Now she seems to have a color complex. The doctor is trying to
associate the colors with something or other. It's way beyond
me. She said she would never wear anything but bright colors
again, and didn't the yellow look pretty with her yellow hair?
Jennie, she had on a short, black full skirt, a black blouse, black
hose and tall red heels. Her hair was bound tightly in a black
scarf. She had on too much make-up and there was a completely
vacant look in her eyes. She twirled around in front of the mirror
wishing that she had a red rose for her hair. She has decided
she will kill her brother, after all. He missed a weekend coming
to see her about a month ago. Of course, it would be impossible
for her to kill a fly. She doesn't even have a spoon in her room."

"Why don't they put her in a state institution since this one
is private and so generous with its rules? You say the inmates
are free to roam around and do about what they wish."

"The doctor said today if she continues to get worse they will
have to, but that her brother wants her to stay there. He must
be rich to pay for all that and to also keep her children in a
private home. The one called Bobby has big doctor bills, too. He
must really be loaded, the brother, I mean."

82

"Who is this brother with all the money? Does he have a wife?" I asked.

"Who he is, only the doctor knows. He is never seen coming or going. He doesn't want it known who he is. Yes, I gather he has a wife, but it's only from conversation. Nobody ever really has said so. But why else would he want it so hush-hush, unless it was to protect his family? If 'protect' is the word. There is still a stigma on any type of mental illness and will be for many years. I know it's like having a sore foot, but the public doesn't think of it in that way."

Ophelia came in, saying, "Did you know that Perry and Bob waited until dark to leave? They were trying to find you, and they have to be in Tulsa at eight o'clock in the morning? Where have you been all day? Where were you?"

"I went to church with you, remember? Then ate lunch with you, remember?"

"Yes, I remember. But where did you spend the afternoon?"

"I was not in, Ophelia, and that is all. I wasn't here. I feel as much like telling you about it as you feel like telling me about Bob. Is that all right?"

She smiled her sweet smile. "Yes, Jennie, that is all right."

"Ophelia, I don't care if Perry never gets back to Tulsa or back to the Vidaurri. He never tells me when he's coming here or when he's leaving. I know men who ask a girl if they can come to see her; he doesn't even tell me. I just don't care."

"They can't help that," she said, still defending Bob. "It's business. That's the way they have to do. They never know; they just come every time they can."

"I think they can help it, Ophelia, and I think that you know it. I think you are trying to see things that are not there — things right in front of your eyes. For instance, why won't Bob fight? In the ranch country that's bad."

She looked startled for a moment and then said quietly as she walked out, "He can't afford to."

She certainly was mixed up — I wondered if she were going to pieces. Everything she said contradicted something else she had said.

I wished Hilda would leave — go on to bed and leave me alone. Toolie was of interest to her, of course, and I could see it was a sad situation, but I had my own sad situation to deal with. I wanted to be left alone.

Hilda was waiting for Carl and working like a dog and trying to show interest in other people. Lee was trying to kill whatever was killing her with gin. Ophelia was dying inside because of something I could not understand, and I was grieving over — was it my children or my parents? No. I was interested in them but my grief was for unrequited love, and I could face it alone. That night, as he was bringing us home, I had tried everything to keep him talking — to prevent his taking me home.

"I have on my pink dress and . . . "

"Jennie, Jennie," he said, "do you think you need to tell me what your dress looks like? You'll have to do better than that if you want to stay here awhile longer. Wrapped in that blanket, I can't see your dress, but it's a light pink, sleeveless, with a little collar, a full pleated skirt, and a big, wide belt. Your heels are too low. Oh, that's none of my business, but all you need is a pair of tall-heeled pink shoes to make it perfect. That wide belt makes your waist look so little. I could almost get my hands around it."

I jerked off the blanket and said, "Want to try?"

He looked out the window and said, "Jennie, don't talk like that. If you keep on — I don't know. Are you warm enough?"

I tried again. "There is one more thing I need to make a perfect costume. I wanted a pink rose to put in my hair tonight, and I wanted to dance with you."

"Oh," he said, "the roses are not real. They make them of pink-red-yellow-white — any color a rose can be and colors that roses sometimes never were — of crepe paper. They only last one evening. If you were a Mexican girl here, in love with a Mexican who works on the ranches, you would probably never have real flowers until the day you married him, and none after that. Most of them can't afford it, and there's something else involved that is not so with your people. Here, a real rose for a dance or a party of any kind is a real thrill to any Mexican girl. It is not just the required sending of a corsage to your date for the party that it is in Chaparral, or any other American town. It's for a very special girl, and it says a very special something you see — not like an engagement ring, no. But more than an American corsage."

I said, "It is also a big thrill to an Anglo girl, to any girl, to get fresh flowers — one or a dozen."

He said, "Perhaps, but it has a different meaning. It's hard to explain. It just means more. It means she is his girl, or he highly respects her, or it may mean he loves her. Only they, the two of them know which."

. . . A very special rose for a very special girl . . . I could believe that would be a very special thrill . . .

Hilda had closed the door to the bedroom when Juan got me out of bed and into the chair. She was sleeping soundly, so that I had to wake her. Juan let us out behind the hotel where he had arranged for Mrs. Gonzales to help Hilda get me up the stairs.

Once more he said, "Stay here, on your side, please."

Hilda and I went to the ranch with Ophelia and Hank for the weekend. The last weekend in November was cool, and the green vegetation was turning brown. We drove just out of Chaparral, just off the main road, onto the widest, smoothest pavement I had been on here.

"My land begins here," Hank said.

It seemed to have no end. He may have had a vague idea where it ended, but in time, we went over fifteen miles of paved road. About a quarter of a mile from the highway, behind a little hill was the house. You came upon it in surprise, like you did coming into Holtville. He said the road went nowhere, just over the ranch, and that he had had it paved because he got tired of trying to miss the holes in the dirt road. Hank was driving the Cadillac slowly and carefully and looked at Ophelia as if he had precious cargo — his own.

The pavement curved, and there was the many-roomed, many-bathroomed, long, low, snowwhite, rambling ranchhouse topped by the ever-present bright red tile.

On the way Hank had told us a little about himself. He had inherited his half of the ranch from his parents. They had been killed, on their horses, just standing in the middle of the little single-gauge railroad track as a cattle train came around the bend. He was only a baby and his Aunt Flora had raised him, there on the ranch. When she and her family moved on, he had stayed there with his great-aunt Sue. Aunt Sue was his father's aunt, and she was old. She liked for young folks to come out to the ranch, but she didn't like to go to town.

Aunt Sue met us at the front gate. After the gate, there was a white picket fence, another gate and this was called "the little yard." We had dinner in a cedar-paneled dining room on a five-hundred dollar table, in a home that must have cost fifty thousand dollars when it was built — and that was at a time when such an amount was a fortune. Glaring lights hung from the ceiling, and we ate off dime store plates with tin knives and forks.

Later, we went with Aunt Sue to feed her chickens. Hilda, Aunt Sue, and I wore old blue jeans and men's old shirts. She could have written a check well into six figures and never missed it, but she did not need anything. She had everything she wanted she said: a good daughter, bringing the children and the grandchildren home to visit, a nice nephew to run the ranch, and work to keep her busy.

"We had a hard time when we wuz young. When Flora wuz a baby, we didn't have no house, but that's right onto sixty years gone. Flora was borned in the cave in that hill over yonder," and she pointed toward the setting sun — pride and memory in her eyes.

"Ranch hadn't been makin' a livin' for Hank's grandpa. Kind of a shiftless feller. Hank's mama and papa, Flora and her man, they got it to workin'. Since they're all gone, we git along, don't we, son?"

You would think, if you did not know, that they were barely getting by.

Hank and Ophelia went riding in the moonlight. Hilda and I walked in the opposite direction. Aunt Sue gave us a lantern and some advice.

"If you git lost, just roll it around three times, right straight up and down and we'll git the signal. Send some o' the hands to git ye."

We walked into the peace and quiet left by the setting sun. Behind us the moon was gliding up over the hill, replacing the sunset purple and gold with silver. It gilded the hilltops and the little pieces of grass and cactus with a faint frost.

"Hank is so quiet and sweet, slow and sort of shy with Ophelia. He's gentle and considerate and thrilled to have her here, and . . . "

Silently I added, "Like Juan."

Hilda said, "Yes, and Ophelia is different here. She is more relaxed and satisfied, not so tense."

We started out to explore the abandoned caves; we got to only one. The cave where Flora had been born was one large room, dug into the side of the hill. They were not caves at all. They were dugouts put here in the days when the man simply married the girl, put her in a wagon, brought her out on the land, and dug her a home. It was warm inside the cave. I think they must have been very happy here. There was no outside opening except the hole through which the first-comers entered their home. There was a large, wooden box in a corner. In it were blankets, a pillow, cooking utensils, a lantern, and further along the wall was a trunk. Evidently, somebody was coming here, using this cave for a hideaway, or a get-away-from-it-all; and the Holts did not know it.

"It's somebody clean," I said. "These things are all clean. It must be a queer duck to hole up in a cave just to get away from whatever he wanted to get away from."

"I'd give anything to dig to the bottom of that box, but I know I shouldn't," Hilda said.

I, too, was dying to do just this.

"Why not? We can put it back like we found it," I urged.

Somehow we managed to talk each other out of it; but we later agreed that if either of us had been alone, she would have done a better job of exploring.

We told Aunt Sue where we had been. I don't know why we did not tell her about the box. She said she was mighty happy in that cave, that she used to sit in the door and hold Flora and look out across the river; hour after hour, she would sit watching for Papa's horse to come over the hills on the Mexican side where he went to roundup cattle.

She added, "On a light night you could see that horse and Papa plain as day on the top of that mountain. You could see all of it — just the way a horse looks and the way the man looks on the horse. Certain times o' night, I can still see it. Nobody been in that cave for forty-fifty years, I guess."

She was a lovely, big, heavy, old pioneer lady remembering and living in her memories.

Hank said, "You girls say the word, and we'll have a dance out here. Got this big ballroom just going to waste."

Ophelia said, "Let's just roam around the ranch and talk."

I did not understand Ophelia. She liked to dance better than any girl I knew. She used to stay upset when Bob did not get in to take her to Lee's dance hall. Early Saturday morning we went swimming in the big, tiled swimming pool. We were splashing about and having fun when Hank called out to me: "Jennie, Perry just called from the Vidaurri. I told him to come on out."

Perry got there about ten. Perry was quiet and calm and not like Bob when he was alone. He did not seem to have so much responsibility; he was more relaxed. He could be himself without having to worry about his boss. What was it about Bob? His being married? Ophelia had been on the defensive about that when I told her I had overheard them talking. I could not figure it out. Hilda and I thought that she was beginning to appreciate Hank more, though.

Perry did not wait. He came immediately to what he wanted. There was no preamble, no waiting to anticipate Bob's wishes as he customarily did. He said, "Hon, let's go somewhere so we can talk." We were sitting on the front porch. When I did not answer, he asked, "Are you warm enough in that little jacket?"

"This is a spring coat, and I'm warm enough. Don't women in Tulsa wear spring coats?"

"No," he said, "they wear fur coats until they put on their bathing suits. You want a fur coat?"

"No," I said, although I had wanted one since I could think.

After this, there was a heavy silence until he said: "I can get here most weekends now, if you want me to."

"Fine," I said.

He said, "How 'bout us gettin' married? Then I won't have to make these long trips."

"I don't want to get married," I said, "not this year. I came here to teach and I'm going to finish the year."

He said, "You're gonna get mighty lonesome, Hon. You will be the only one left of the Vidaurri girls, in no time."

"They will all be there," I told him.

"No," he said, "Hilda will marry Carl this month, or any month he gets here. Lee may marry Bunk if he keeps after her. He's got it bad. You watch what I tell you, if you stay here you'll be all alone long before your school ends."

"Well, go ahead. Where is Ophelia going?"

"I'm just telling you you'll be the only one here."

When I asked him why Bob had not come with him, he looked off into the little blobs of sand that were whirling among the mesquites and said, "He has no business here any more. Ophelia was his only reason for stopping here and that's over."

"Who did it?" I asked.

"I don't know," he said.

Sunday morning Hank said, "Let's all take a long walk."

We knew that he wanted to show Ophelia where Aunt Sue had lived when she was a bride. Hilda and I would have liked to stop it; I guess we wanted to get into that box after all. However, it was Hank's ranch, and he could do whatever he wanted, so we went along.

"What's this?" Hank said, when he saw the box and he began to lift things out of it. A letter fell out of the fold in the second blanket. It flipped onto its back side and before he could turn it over, Ophelia said:

"Put it back. It isn't yours. Put it back, it isn't yours."

On and on like a broken record she repeated the words. Hank stood foolishly with the letter face down in his hand. It had fallen out of the blanket. He made no move to open it. He had no intention of reading it. He put it back under the blanket where it had been.

Perry said, "Somebody is sure trespassing on your property, Hank. I'd do something about that. Isn't that a serious offense?"

"No, well, yes I guess it is, if you want to push it, but I never do. Caves, little holes dug in the sides of the hills, are all over all the ranches around here. People from town come out here when they want to get away from their jobs, or anything.

It's warm in the winter and cool in the summer. Why, some of our leading citizens use these caves as weekend homes. I don't care."

Ophelia kept looking at the blanket as if it were a snake, and she the snake charmer. Her face was drained of all color and her eyes were big and black. I thought they looked frightened. She was as still and silent as a statue. Stooping, we left the cave by way of the little door, and I looked back just as Ophelia put the letter into her purse!

Outside, Ophelia became physically ill. Hank almost carried her across the valley to the ranch house, and Aunt Sue put her to bed. She kept bringing coffee, the ranch cure for colds, hot weather, blues, fatigue, despair, too much or too little of anything; but it was sometime before Ophelia felt up to driving back to town.

On the way in, Perry asked, "Hank, do you know who Juan Ortega is?"

Ophelia answered, "Yes, he's a Mexican who has a cafe in Little Mexico."

Hank said, "New man there. Nobody knows where he came from or anything about him — bad reputation. Pretty fast with the women, I hear. College man. Thinks he knows it all. College ruins 'em. Them Mexicans."

Ophelia said vehemently to Hank, "You don't know a thing in the world about that man, so don't repeat all you hear. It could all be false. Don't run that man down, or I'll never come here again."

Ophelia was upset all out of proportion to the event. Hank said slowly and softly, "Honey, I'll never say another word about that man. You're right, I don't know a thing in the world about him."

Ophelia said quietly, "Jennie can tell you what kind of a man he is."

Then she turned and looked at me in the back seat in apology and disbelief at having said this. She had not known she was going to say it. I knew that she —that they all — knew. I felt sick.

Perry said, "All right, Hon. You tell us about this Mexican." His eyes were coals of fire, but his voice was quiet and controlled. Too quiet.

90

"I suppose she means that Juan Ortega is a friend of mine. He is a nice fellow."

"But who is he?" Perry insisted.

Ophelia said, "You wouldn't understand, Perry. He's a middle-class Mexican who makes a decent living. He lives a decent life and has a one-hundred per cent pure heart."

"That's the fellow who wanted to eat in Lee's," Perry said as if he had just put it together.

"No," I said, "he ordered a ham sandwich to take out."

When we got to the Vidaurri, it was dark; and I did not want to be alone in the dark with Perry. I said, "I'm going home."

Perry said, "All right, Hon, but it's early yet. Let's sit in the park a little while, then I'll take you home and be on my way back to Tulsa."

"I don't want to stay at the Vidaurri. I want to go home."

He told me, "I tried to get you to go home before you got all messed up. You said no, you didn't have a home; you had no people; the Vidaurri was your home. Now, I'm trying to get you to go to Tulsa, and you want to go to Musgrove. Stay here now. It's not time to leave."

"For anywhere but Tulsa?"

"For anywhere but Tulsa."

Ophelia was out with Hank almost every night after that. She was quiet, calm, and thoroughly miserable, we thought. Somewhere in the transfer from Bob to Hank, she had lost her sparkle and her spark. She was working toward something, like a woman with a purpose; but she had gone far away from us, mentally. She appeared to be lost in her own world, with life — stilled and waiting — showing in her eyes.

Mrs. Luz called me Sunday evening at the Vidaurri and invited me to her home for coffee after school on Monday. She must have decided to teach me Spanish after all. It would be no problem; I would simply go to her house. There had been no talk — that I knew of — of my going to visit the parents. Certainly, there should be none if I went to her house for Spanish lessons. I had picked up a few words from Mrs. Gonzales' efforts and a few from the children, but I could not make a complete sentence. What an opportunity this would be! I could hardly wait until after school Monday.

Mrs. Luz served coffee and little cakes, and then she started talking.

"I should like to tell you a little about myself and about the Mexican people before I — ah — make any suggestions," she said.

Oh, wonderful . . . she's going to offer something for the Mexicans . . . some way she can help through me.

Mrs. Luz was a statuesque, handsome woman with the pale skin and large grey eyes and the long black hair of the Spanish. She wore her hair dressed in a huge bun at the back of her neck, straight and severe. She was wearing a simple, expensive, black dress with large, hand-wrought Mexican jewelry. There was one huge diamond beside her wedding ring. She was not smiling. She was courteous, dignified, and entirely proper — old style Spanish proper.

She said, "We have our home in Mexico City, and our people have lived there for many generations. My husband and I never lived anywhere else until we came here. He wanted to be a medical missionary, and when he grew determined to come here, I left my home, my friends and my very way of life to come with him."

I looked around her lovely home. It was probably a shack compared to the home she spoke of in Mexico City. Through a hall I could see a clothes closet that seemed to go on forever. It was filled to over-flowing with expensive dresses, dresses only. Jewelry was spilling out of boxes, even in the living room. I could not see that she had made too great a sacrifice; so I waited.

"We left our two daughters at our home. They are attending the university there. We — that is, I — would not subject them to the humiliation and degradation of coming here.

After searching for something to say, and finding nothing adequate, I came up with, "You can be anything you want to be, anywhere in the world."

"Oh, no, Miss Camish. I, too, once thought so. I have friends in Holtville with whom I play bridge. We play in their homes and in my little home here. I read a great deal. That is all there is for me to do. There is no one with whom I care to associate here. Even my sister-in-law doesn't approve of me. She is a self-appointed missionary. She thinks I should be, but I am not the type." Her expression invited comment so I fumed inside and tried.

"I knew that Brother Luz is Doctor Luz's brother," I stopped. We both were silent, so I said: "Mrs. Luz, you asked me here for some reason. Are you ready to tell me what it is?"

"There are various types of people in any race, yours, mine, and all others. There are the lowest, most poverty-stricken, and uneducated; and there are the highest, most highly educated, cultured, moneyed people, and there are those in between."

The room was getting stuffy, and my clothing was too tight, suddenly. But my throat wouldn't open. Only my mouth opened.

"Leave Juan Ortega alone!" Her dignity had suddenly left her. She had held herself in check as long as she could. Her eyes were big and a bitter green. "He was a wonderful and well-adjusted young man before you started to work on him. He was the only person in all of Little Mexico with whom I could carry on an intelligent conversation. He already has had trouble enough to last his lifetime. Then *you* came over here, and luck fell into your lap. You used a trumped-up pain in your ankle to get in with him. I know; my husband told me you were not injured. Now, you tell me, why would an Anglo girl contrive to spend the night with a Mexican man?"

I said, "I'll tell you nothing, Mrs. Luz. You're doing the talking. You tell me."

She did not hesitate to do so. "There could be only one reason," she said. "Now, is there any difference in Mexican love and American love?" Her voice was a snarl.

Juan, oh Juan, you tried to tell me what they would think.

"Mrs. Luz," I began.

"One moment. You are playing at helping what you call the downtrodden, and you are doing a beautiful job of it. It is working! Never have you wanted anything for your 'little ones' that Juan didn't get it. Miss Camish wants; Miss Camish gets. Well, let me tell you something else, young lady, something that you *will* be interested in. Juan Ortega is not a wealthy man. He is gradually spending what he has, and he cannot be making a living in that cafe. He is giving all he makes away and, whatever your game, you're doomed to lose. You can't get money where there isn't any. When the novelty wears off, where will you go?"

I had worn my red dress and red shoes and the red beads all day. They were the best clothing I had. I had worn them to come and listen to this. My clothes were wet; I was wet all over.

"Have you finished? Mrs . . .

"No, I have not. That man is a wreck, and it's your doing. Nobody knows where he goes, but he leaves here for several days at a time — on weekends when your American boy friend is at the hotel with you. When he returns, he looks as if he has been through the depths of grief. I won't have it! Why do you do it? Work on the American. You'll never get anywhere with Juan. Leave him alone. LEAVE MY PEOPLE ALONE," she screamed as she walked toward the door.

I said, "Sit down Mrs. Luz. I am not ready to go. You invited me here, and I hardly think your Mexican protocol would let you invite me out."

"Oh, but it will," she said. "Mexican protocol doesn't go *that* far."

"Mrs. Luz, if you put me out of your house I will stand in your front yard and scream for all Little Mexico to hear what I have to say. I listened to you; now you listen to me."

She sat down.

"You know why your sister-in-law doesn't care for you. It's because you're not human. You have three Mexican women working in your house right now. They are what you call low class. I know all of them. Your little finger is not worth all three of them. They have no money and no education, but they have love and faith — things you don't know anything about. You don't know what love is."

She screamed, "I have a husband and two daughters, and I don't know what love is?"

I told her: "Married love and the love for your own children, perhaps. That is only one kind of love. Did you ever watch a tiny little girl turn from being a mass of fear and trembling and shrinking and become a carefree, happy little girl who tried to get to you first so she could rub up against you like a kitten?

94

Did you ever look down into her eyes and see the love and trust and the warmness and the answer to unknown longings there? Did you know that this took patience and effort and time, to awaken this little girl? No, you don't know this because you didn't do any of this, Mrs. Luz. You have never given wholly of yourself without expectation of something in return. This is the true love. You speak of your 'sacrifices.' I doubt if you have ever sacrificed anything in your life. Now, I'll tell you a little about me before I make any — ah — suggestions."

"I want nothing," she said. "I know all I want to know about you."

"If you put me out I'll scream all the way down the mountain, after you have the police pick me up, Mrs. Luz," I threatened; and when I saw she was listening, I continued:

"I am what you would call low class. I have no money, no background and have never had much of either. I have very little education. One year of college, and I got that by working and borrowing money. I have no culture as I understand your definition. I do not know how to play bridge very well. I have never been to the opera. I have never in all of my life seen what you would call first-class entertainment. I have only a goal —

"That I know," she interrupted. "I know your goal, but Juan Ortega would never have you permanently. He comes from a very fine background. My family has known his family for many years, though I myself don't know them. We have our goals, too, and our standards. They are not low. Change your aim. Go to your own people."

"Sit down," I told her. She was standing, white and furious. "You told me to leave your people alone. What have you ever done for them? For your people? Dr. Luz works alone." I pointed to the dresses. "You have enough money tied up in clothes alone to send half the kids in Little Mexico to college, but you're above associating with 'your people.' Yet, you tell me to leave them alone. I've heard the Anglos who didn't know your people run them down, but I've never known people to run down their own race, or any other race as you have just done. You tell me, in effect, to 'let my people go.' Go where, Mrs. Luz? Always under? Always to be under subjection? To never have an opportunity to do better than they do? Oh, what you could do for these people if you only wanted to!"

95

"These people are neither my affair nor yours. We have our own missionaries. We could get one to come —"

"But they are not here. I am. And I intend to stay."

"You are a very stubborn young woman."

I admitted that I was. She asked me to have more coffee and cake, and I told her the food was choking me. She sat down again, trying to control herself. I stood in front of her.

"Mrs. Luz, you stay up here on top of your hill in your nice home with your nice jewelry and furniture and clothes. You isolate yourself from the 'lowest class' — your people. Well, live in your aloneness and your bitterness and your aristocratic background. Let nothing contaminate you, but LEAVE ME ALONE. I care a great deal what the Mexican people think of me — the good, decent, giving, loving, trying Mexican people. I don't give a dime what you think of my past, present, or future. Whatever my future becomes, you can be assured that you had nothing to do with it. I won't discuss Juan Ortega with you for two reasons: one, you have firmly convinced yourself of our relationship. Nothing I could say would change that; and, since I don't care, it wouldn't be worth the effort. The second reason," I stopped abruptly, "the other reason is my own," I said softly.

She looked at me very strangely as I started to leave, and then she said, "That is a lovely speech. You must have said it many times. In the end it will get you nowhere. I see one other reason, other than Juan, why you are contented to work with the low class; you are one of them."

"That I am," I answered.

I was almost too weak and spent to walk, but I had to get to my car. I walked slowly trying not to show how emotionally affected I was, how my knees were shaking. I was afraid to drive, but I went very slowly hoping I could get to the bottom of the hill, and soon I was in my classroom, sitting at my desk, with my head in my hands.

Was Juan really broke? Had I made him sick? I had contrived to see him, but I had thought that he, too, cared. Was I really killing the soul of a wonderful man? Should I leave him alone? Why was Mrs. Luz so upset and so bitter? Was it only because the Anglos would not associate with her? I had wanted so much to know her. I had thought she could help, and now I knew she hated me enough to kill me. If I were to marry Perry, they would all shut up — the Anglos wouldn't start talking against the Mexicans every time they saw me. Life would be simple and normal if I married Perry, and maybe that was the thing I should do. I was so tired — so very tired.

My head began to ache, and my eyes blurred. I was too weak to go on to the Vidaurri. I wished I could just sleep here tonight — that I did not have to face anybody. I put my head down on my desk, and I do not know how long I had been there when Juan came quietly in through the door.

"Jennie," he asked, "are you all right?"

He had seen the light in the classroom from the cafe. I raised my head, but my glazed eyes could not focus.

"You are not all right," he said. "You are ill. What is it? Tell me."

He said he had seen me go to the Luz home after school, and that he had watched to see when I came back. He saw me stop at the school, but waited awhile to come over. He did not know why I had stopped. Finally, he had become worried.

"What happened up there? What did she say? What did she do to you? Tell me!" He demanded, and he shook me by my shoulders. I responded like a rag doll. He squatted by the desk chair and took both my hands in his.

"Ah, Jennie, tell me. Please, tell me."

"Es nada," I said, and it was the first time I had said a word in Spanish without planning to do so.

"We're not having a Spanish lesson tonight," he said. "Tell me, Jennie. I must know."

"I can't tell you, ever," I said. "But, Juan I never meant to hurt you. If I ever have, I'm sorry. I'll leave you alone, Juan. Like you always wanted me to. Go back to the cafe and I'll leave you alone. I promise, Juan. I'll never bother you again."

He looked as if he did not know what to do or say, now that I had promised to leave him alone.

"Ah, Jennie," he said with the Spanish pronunciation, "I have never — I will never *want* you to leave me alone. I knew, and I know it's the only way. Can't you tell me what happened?"

"No," I said.

I was reasonably certain that Mrs. Luz would not tell him,

and the Mexican women who worked for her would be afraid to talk about it.

"I am in enough trouble already, just as you told me I would be," I said. "I don't want any more trouble. I can't stand any more trouble. I've done everything I could think of to get you Juan, and it must be wrong. I guess I''m the only person who ever thought it was right, so it must be wrong. You go with Angelita and I'll go with Perry. I'll stay on my side like you always told me to."

He said, "Jennie, you have never hurt me. Any hurt I feel is because of myself, because I feel for you what I do. You couldn't have stopped it Jennie, no matter what you tried. You had, and never will have, any control over the way I feel toward you. It just is that way. You are not to blame."

For a moment I did not move. Then I stood up intending to leave.

"Jennie, before you go, I want to tell you that I love you as I never have and never could love another woman," he said.

"I know that," I replied calmly. "I've known that all along. That's what has made it so hard, but you were right all the time."

He kissed me. It was the first time, and he kissed my lips and then my cheeks, and my eyes as if he were healing the bruise of a child.

"Whatever Maria Luz said or did to you, it is not worth suffering over. You must know, now, that all she has is money."

"Yes, I know that now," I said.

He said more: "No person of any race is worth what you're suffering; least of all, Maria Luz."

Juan wanted to call Hilda to come after me, but I objected. As he put me into my car, he said, "Jennie, you can do better than Perry. An Anglo, yes, but not Perry. There are single ranchers and oil boys all over the county. Go with somebody else."

"No, Perry is all right," I said. "I know him, and I don't feel like exerting the effort of even meeting another man. You said an Anglo, remember."

"Always, I'll remember, but not that one. Will you remember that always I'll love you?"

"Yes, always, I'll know that," I said.

EIGHT

SLOWLYI drove to the Vidaurri, without interest and without purpose. I did not want to go to bed. Bert and Lou were sitting in the lobby.

Bert said, "Jennie, we never see you any more. Why don't you come to see us?" He smiled and added, "I know, too many Mexicans and Perry, and waiting for Perry. He's a nice fellow, and he's crazy about you. Why don't you go ahead and marry him? Then you wouldn't have to put up with those Mexican kids. Oh, I know you 'love them,' but married life is the only life."

He took his wife's hand as he smiled at her.

I said, "I'm just tired, Bert."

Lou said, "You and Perry haven't had any trouble have you? You look so pale."

"No," I said, "we haven't had any trouble. I'm just worn out, been too busy."

I felt that I had to get away from there, and as I walked out the door I heard Bert say, "Do you suppose she and Perry broke up? Somehow she looks sick."

"No, I don't think so," replied Lou. "He's here all the time; seems devoted to her. Ophelia and Bob certainly got over whatever it was they had for each other in a hurry, didn't they?"

"Yes," Bert said. "I thought for a while they were going to get married, but now it seems it's Hank Holt. But Ophelia doesn't look exactly happy, does she?"

Lou said, "Honey, there are things going around and around all about us, and we have no idea, but I do know there is something. I guess they think we're getting too old to confide in."

Cava said, "That Miss Jennie, she don't look so good. I wonder what the matter is. I wonder did she and Mr. Perry, they fall out?"

Lou said, "Cava, stop listening in, and don't talk."

"Oh, no 'me," he said. "I never say I word I not 'sposed to say, Miss Lou."

I went to Lee's and ordered coffee. Lee was talking to Bunk.

"No, you're not going to get into that poker game either. I don't care if you are behind. You can just stay behind. Now, sit down and eat that sandwich."

Bunk looked as if he were a child with a new toy.

"Well, sure, Baby. I won't play poker if you don't want me to. I didn't know you cared."

"Well, maybe I don't," she said, "but you've got me to change my whole life. You ought to have to do something. I can't drink gin anymore. I can't talk loud. I can't use much make-up. Even got the red going off my hair. Can't even talk about them filthy . . . "

"Easy does it, Lee. There's Jennie."

Lee's hair was a pretty shade of brown where the part showed. It looked terrible with the dye wearing off, but you could see that she might be pretty when she got the dye off and quit putting on so much make-up.

After school on Friday, the note was in the contorted mirror where Mrs. Gonzales put my daily Spanish word. The note was in a sealed envelope with my name typed on the outside. The note was typewritten and unsigned. I read: "Any day now the police will announce the name of the murderer. It will not be the right one, but that cannot be proved. There is nothing to worry about. Never let anyone know where you were that night. You must keep out of this."

On Friday night, Ophelia and Hank and Perry were sitting at the end of the veranda in the comfortable wicker chairs when Hilda came up. She said to Ophelia, "I picked up the Sunday

100

school quarterlies in Holtville. I knew Hank was in town."

Ophelia smiled sadly and removed her hand from Hank's.

"I'm glad you are all here," she said. "You're all the people I want to talk to and I will only have to tell it this one time." She turned to Perry. "You know Bob always said I could tell this if and when I chose?"

"Yes, but are you sure — ?"

"I never was so sure of anything in my life. Hank asked me to marry him, and he has told all of you, so I'm not breaking a confidence."

Hank said, "You're sho' right there, Honey."

"There's nothing I'd rather do than spend the rest of my life with Hank Holt." Ophelia did not look at Hank. She looked back at the hill. Then she went on. "But, I can't." For a moment all was silence as we waited for her to go on. "I'll tell one of the reasons why he won't want to marry me, the reason why I think I'll never marry anybody."

Hank said, "Ophelia, Honey," and reached for her hand.

As she withdrew it, she said "I'm sick and tired of my Vidaurri friends thinking what you all think of Bob and of me. Bob and I won't see each other again, and I want this cleared. Bob is not, and has never been, married. He has a sister who is mentally ill. She's in a private rest home. She has five children in a private home. Bob pays all the bills. It is too much expense without adding me." She looked at Hank. "He told me this. He said that he couldn't afford me. I offered to support myself. Even then, he didn't want me. I don't want to marry Bob, now. I can never marry anybody."

Hank tried to tell her none of this made any difference to him. He insisted he wanted to marry her.

"What's the sister's name?" Hilda asked as if she were afraid to hear it.

"Alma. That's all I know. I never asked."

"Where is she?"

"I never asked that either."

"Where is her husband?"

"She doesn't have a husband, Hilda. I am sure this wouldn't come under the head of social work," Ophelia said and smiled her sad smile.

Hank said, "Baby, that makes no difference to me."

Ophelia said, "You're the nicest man I've ever met, and now I am going to bed."

After she left, we all sat there quietly. There seemed nothing to say. We had, all except Perry, expected the worst, and I felt that guilt-ridden feeling all over again for listening to their talk.

Perry added some information: "Bob could get off as often as he did only to see his sister. He tried to make it on weekends. I could come with him because of my job. That is how we were able to ever come to the Vidaurri."

Perry looked at me and said, "Ophelia knew we really couldn't know when we were coming here or when we would have to leave. It was always so sudden — when Alma would need Bob, or want him. I wanted to tell you, Jennie, but Bob wouldn't hear of it. It's been hard trying to convince you when I had my hands tied. Bob didn't want Ophelia to tell this. He thought it would be better for the children if it did not get out. He . . . "

Hilda interrupted with a great deal of vehemence: "He thought it would be better for Bob. He didn't seem to be worried about Ophelia's reputation. What do you think we all thought? What would you think?"

"I'm sure Bob didn't think of it that way."

"No, Bob thought of Bob."

I asked Hilda to leave it for now.

Perry said, "You see, Hank, if Bob got into any trouble, like a fight or anything and the word got around, they would find out he had not spent all of his time with his sister. Bob is not a bad guy. He let himself look bad in order to be with Ophelia. Now, that she doesn't want him . . . "

Hank said, "I just hope you're right, because I intend to marry that girl, somehow, somewhere, sometime."

Perry said, "I think you will."

Perry asked me if I wanted to go to Lee's. I answered, "No, I just want to go to bed."

Hank said he didn't, somehow, feel like playing poker tonight and he never did like to dance, so he believed he would

102

just go to bed. That left Perry and me still sitting in the wicker chairs, alone.

Perry said, "Jennie, will you marry me?"

You can't tell a thing about people by the way they look. Hank looks as if he would have to borrow a nickle or a dime, if he went into Holtville to buy a hamburger. He begins to look different the minute he saunters out to get in his Cadillac and drive off. Tall and thin and indefinite features that make him look no way in particular, but nice and sincere, and in no way a good-looking man. The boots and spurs and tight pants begin to look sharp — in the Cadillac, they do. If you did not know Hank Holt, you would be shocked to see him get into the car. Hank Holt was a good man, a rare man; and we were just finding it out.

Juan, now, looks like a graduate student in a big university; not quite a businessman, but past the college boy stage. They are the same, tall, thin, slow-moving, but there the likeness stops. He is so very dark that we would all look blond beside him. No wonder he thinks I am a blonde.

Perry — Perry just looks like an oil boy, clean, starched, faded, hard-pressed suit of khakis; but you can imagine an oil boy a sharp dresser. They can be, you know. You know what he would look like in dress clothes, except that, in the ranch country you never see him in anything but khakis. It would have to be something very special to get him in dress clothes.

Bob looks like Perry. You'd imagine or know they were oil boys anywhere in Texas. But nobody could even imagine Hank in evening clothes. He would ruin the effect by wearing cowboy boots and a ten-gallon hat. He would never be classed as well-dressed, but his wife would. She would be among the best dressed women of the world. That is where he gets his pride. She is his ad. She bespeaks the fact that he is successful. That is the way he wants it. The oil boy is fond of himself, too. He wants to be able to be well-dressed when he is in the mood. He likes his wife to be dressed well first, but he is going to dress up, too. Hank is simple and plain and giving and in love. Perry is — I don't know.

"No, I mean I don't know. I don't think I do. Like Ophelia says 'I don't think I'll marry anybody.'"

He said, "I'll ask you again."
Too much was happening too fast. I went to bed.

He asked me again the next morning. I suppose he asked me again.

"Do you want to spend the rest of your life here fighting for a useless cause, or do you want to spend your life with me in Tulsa?"

I told him I wanted breakfast.

Ophelia and Hank were just going into Lee's. We joined them. The three-piece orchestra was playing at Miss Gorman's request and she was singing. She had never sung anything but church music and we had always wanted her to. She was singing and beating time on the table. The song was "Blues In The Night." She was making a strong effort to be cheerful and all this with tears in her voice made it a terrific rendition.

Lee said she could pay her a pile o' money to sing upstairs on Saturday nights and Bunk said, "You stay out of this, Baby," and she hushed.

Bert and Lou came in. Bert said, "Well, now, this looks better, seeing a group of happy young people together. These girls have been looking sort of unhappy lately; always like to see you boys here. Things cheer up."

Carl's latest letter said he might not get in until January. After all, they were busy. Hilda said her blue dress would still be new to Carl. She knew he was coming, and she could wait. There was never doubt in Hilda — never.

In Little Mexico, they were building the dance palace. It looked sturdier, but was going up fast. Occasionally, I would see Juan walking around over the pile of lumber and working with the men. He was just across the street and up the little hill, but he never once looked my way.

Pedro was in school. He could sing three songs all the way through, and last Sunday he had sung "What a Friend We Have in Jesus" in the Mexican Baptist Mission in Holtville. He was the proudest boy I ever saw. He sang it for a week, in the classroom and on the playground.

Hilda was working most of the time in Holtville. Lee was

104

drinking coffee or sitting in the little park with her coat on, talking to Bunk about the future, or so we thought. The brown streak in her hair was getting nearer the ends and it was pretty. She was not running the Mexicans down — except when Bunk was not around, and he had to work part of the time.

Ophelia was spending her evenings with Hank. She still looked unhappy and undecided, but she went out with him. She came in one night to talk to me; I didn't know then that she was telling me anything, but she was. She said, "A cowboy song is a lament of great sadness and loneliness. It's a wandering and a searching — always wandering the vast reaches over which he rides his horse. It's in a minor key, with the rhythm matching the empty spaces and the job of the horse and the heart of the cowboy. It's the mood that the West was built on."

I was beginning to understand — a little. "Yes," I said. "They often had to sing to hear a human voice. At first, there were no women, then a very few women, and some of them weren't of the highest type, to put it mildly. The song would naturally be one of loneliness and longing. The cowboy was alone — always, very much alone."

"Sure," she said, "that was the reason. The rest of the world may make fun of our music, but Texas-Mexican border music is as surely folk music as is, 'Annie Laurie.' And, Jennie, if you're born to it, I mean on either side of the river, when you listen you get a sort of nostalgic longing — a passionate longing for — something. You may not know for what, or why, but you get this. You keep searching and one day, maybe, you find it. They ride the range in Fords, Cadillacs and pickup trucks now; and they drive to the Vidaurri on weekends; but they sing the same songs the early settlers sang; the mood is still there. The feel of the music is born in you. I think the Mexicans feel it just as the Americans do. We must feel the same. But, sometimes, I get the music mixed. I mean I forget which is Mexican and which is cowboy — or is it all one?"

The morning light was behind her hair, making it look a deep brown, with big blobs of dark blue. Her face looked at you soft and sweet. Maybe it was the memory of the music. She kept talking as if she would never be either tired or sleepy. I tried to tell her I felt all that about the music but that I could never have put it into words.

They must have been desperately lonely, the first settlers.

"They knew a loneliness we'll never know, Jennie. My grandmother told me — she's very old now — about the long nights of waiting and hoping: waiting for her father, waiting with her mother, and after a while, of waiting for her husband to come home. It's all very vague," she said and left the room abruptly.

After our talk that vague, mixed-up longing kept coming back to me. It was a physical thing in its intensity; and, yet, there was something definitely not physical about it. I was searching, and the craving was so strong that I was divided between impulse and common sense. But not for long.

My emotional impulses always took over when the yearning became strong and heavy. I would be at school, or walking through the lobby, or just anywhere, doing anything, or nothing and the yearning — for what I did not know — would take over and steal my poise and my stability and any shred of common sense I may have had.

I could not get rid of the feeling, and I could not find the answers to so many things. I did not know that the answers would come later, with age and time, and that I should not hurry them. Nobody told me. They did not know how.

I knew I always wanted to see Juan. Hilda and Ophelia must have known it, too. Everytime I walked out of the room, one of them joined me. I realized they did not enjoy my company all of the time, but I could not get ten feet from the lobby without someone joining me. I couldn't get to Juan.

The week before we dismissed school for Christmas was cold and damp. The hills were bare and brown except for the green patches dotted here and there. Mrs. Gomez and her husband brought us a Christmas tree, a short, dumpy pine that had lived its short life in the mountains of New Mexico. The children decorated it with colored paper chains, bits of tinsel, and bright colored scraps. It looked like an over-dressed, short, dumpy little woman; we loved it.

We drew names for Christmas. The party was much the same as children's Christmas parties everywhere, but the gifts were cheaper — cheaper and more expensive with love and the joy of

106

giving. The mothers joined in as we sang, with Pedro leading the singing. They sang the carols Ophelia had taught them, in English. Then, for me, they sang "Silent Night" in Spanish. They did not know it had been originally written in German and that now it belonged to the world, in any language. They knew it was their Christmas song.

NINE

AFTER
the school day was over, Pedro stayed. He came up to my desk
and said that he had been out of school because he went to the
funeral of his aunt in Mexico with his papa. He said they sang a
song like "We Gather the River" and did I know it? He asked if
this meant we will all meet at our river some day when we go to
heaven. With round, big eyes, a few inches from mine, with big
brown fist grasping onto the edge of my desk, he waited with
bated breath for the answer.

Ah, my little boy:
We shall gather at the river means . . . Our Father who art
in Heaven . . . what do I say now? It is a great river — the River
of God . . . perhaps it is not a place . . . only a hope that we may
be together throughout eternity . . . or it may be the way you
live . . . the way you believe . . . it is . . . Ah, Pedro, the question
it too profound and the answer too deep for me to answer.

"Yes, Pedro," I said, "it means if we live good lives and
trust God and do everything we think is right, that someday we
will all be together in happiness."

He appeared to think that over for a while, then he asked,
"If we could not find the river, I mean if it is not in heaven,
then what would we do?"

"We would know the way. We would follow the rainbow . . . "

Juan was standing in the door, saying only to me, "To our

108

pot of dreams, that we will find only when we have no river to cross; only at the end of the rainbow, and that will be never."

The children were running down the dusty road with their packages and all the colored paper and ribbon and strings that had been used to tie the packages.

Juan said, "We will have a party for the children and the parents next Wednesday after school. I think it will be all right for you to come if you bring Hilda with you, and go home before dark."

He had moved the tables along the sides of the room to make room for games and dancing. The games and folk dancing were a mixture of English that they had learned at home and that Ophelia and I had taught them. The joy of Christmas was the same joy one sees in the eyes of children everywhere. The piñata came apart amid yells of glee and the sounds that tiny brown feet made scrambling around on the floor for the candies and little favors, all the things that had been in the big, paper donkey.

Juan stood, leaning against the wall, relaxed, slack in every line of his body, as if this were his world. Slanty eyes merry for once, and handsome with his white, even teeth showing through his slightly parted lips. His smile was sweet as if he knew a secret.

I walked over to him. "I don't understand why you refused to allow Ophelia to come to this party! You'd think, from your attitude that if she had come here she would be committing a crime." I was angry and my voice showed it. "She has Pedro singing solos in church. She has all the children doing American folk dances. She is working now to form a quartet of little boys. What do you have against her?"

"I have nothing against Miss Gorman." Juan's expression did not change. Every person in the cafe was watching us for any slight change, and we both knew it. "I wanted you to come because it would make the parents and the children happy. I wanted Miss Smaltz to come so that you would not have to drive home alone. That is all. One extra Anglo is all you need to make it all right for you to be here."

Without another word and without waiting for me to reply,

Juan began a Mexican version of the Apache dance. With complete abandon he took the center of the floor, and Mr. Morin gently pushed Mrs. Morin toward Juan as he danced toward them. Mrs. Morin closed her eyes, twisted her body, threw her head back and started around Juan in the slinking step that is basic to the adagio. I felt that for her there was no today, nor tomorrow. She was mentally a thousand years in the past. For her all the long yesterdays were alive: Indian and Mexican, the Aztec Chief, Montezuma — whatever was mixed in her blood, little, if any, was Anglo. No Anglo could learn to dance this way, to this degree of intensity, in only one little lifetime. I would have given a great deal to be in Mrs. Morin's place tonight.

The Morins had once been a professional dance team and a good one. During the many intricate steps of the dance Juan deftly released Mrs. Morin to her husband, and so the dance began. The Morins were still good. During the dance they escaped from our world as they had not been able to do in their marriage. But, there was still the strong pull — too strong to break. It was in their one body, one love, one life movement. Their eyes were mere slits, and I think that only they could know the depths of their thoughts.

. . . This dance says everything that I have tried to say to you, Juan . . . It says, "I love you, I want you, I surrender; no, I don't. Now, you chase me. You'll never catch me. Yes, I will let you catch me. Come here. Go away. I am out of your reach forever. Now, I melt at your feet." . . . I have used all the words and wiles I can think of to say these things . . . I think we have both said them . . . throughout we said or did these things that indicated "come here" or "go away."

Juan did not look at me. He danced only that one time to get the dancing started. The orchestra was a group from Holtville and the couples began ballroom dancing after the adagio.

The children are so polite: the little boy puts his left arm, from the elbow to the wrist, behind the small of his back, palm out. He puts his right arm the same way, across his midriff, palm in. He bows stiffly from the waist, and as he stands he extends the crook of his elbow to the little girl, who softly, as light as a whisper, puts her little hand into the crooked elbow. He leads

110

her onto the floor and holds her very gently and not very close. He brings her back to her mama at the end of the dance and thanks them both. She smiles at him.

These are my children, but I did not teach them this. They learned this instinctively; it is a part of their heritage; they have known the procedure, with all its delicate graces, for centuries. I may teach them English, to jump rope, to use their napkins and not to eat with the fingers; and I may teach them many things, but never could I teach them the ease and dignity and grace with which they perform this ritual.

I could never learn to do it with the ease that they display either. The Anglo is born with many things of the past that some other races do not have, but he is not born with the primitive dance, or its ease and grace running in his blood for generations passed.

. . . Mrs. Luz, this is your low class, uneducated people; without money, without culture . . . These are your people . . . I wish you could see them tonight, or could you see them as they really are if you were here? "Let my people go," you said . . . They are going to best you Mrs. Luz . . . "We Shall Gather at the River," and I wonder if you know I did LEAVE JUAN ORTEGA ALONE . . . I wonder if you are very happy about this . . . Merry Christmas, Mrs. Luz . . .

Juan was looking at me as though he could read my mind and then, his eyes mere slits, he was looking beyond me. One of the men in the orchestra was coming in my direction. Juan said something to him and he went back to the orchestra.

"Miss Camish, you and Miss Smaltz go home now."

"Oh, no," Hilda objected, "this is fun."

He said, very low. "Jennie, go home now."

Hilda and I drove to the hotel. Juan followed us, and as we got out of the car I saw his red Buick turn around and head back toward Little Mexico. It was the only place in the world I really wanted to be tonight.

The first thing I saw in my room was the bracelet — old, handmade of silver, with ornate cutting on it. The note said, "I can afford this. I am neither as broke as Maria Luz would have you believe, nor as rich as some of the other Mexican people

111

believe. Merry Christmas." Inside the bracelet, on a narrow metal band, was engraved "Feliz Navidad, 12-21-40."

By January of 1941, there was much talk of war. It did not seem important to us that people were fighting somewhere on the other side of an ocean. If it did not happen in our little world, it did not touch us. Perry called me on Friday night and asked if he might come to the Vidaurri about six on Saturday afternoon. He had never before asked me anything; he had only told me, or had just come without telling me.

He arrived a little before six. He was well-dressed in a navy blue suit, and I was surprised. I had never seen him in anything but khakis. We went to Lee's for dinner. He was not drinking, and when someone asked him to join them in a fast one he said, "No, thanks, fellers. I'm not drinking tonight. No, no poker either; just came to see my girl."

This was a new approach.

"Jennie," he said, "let's go back to that same corner of the veranda where Ophelia told us about Bob." Perry smiled nervously which was unlike him. "Futures seem to be decided in that corner, and I came here tonight to settle mine."

When we were settled in the wicker chairs he said, "I know you don't like drinking or poker playing. A married man does not need to do either."

"Nobody has to do either," I said.

"No, but a single guy, just running around, you do. It's something you do. I know how you want to live. I'll go to church with you. I'll buy you a home in Tulsa. I've got a pretty good job. I mean, well, I'll come home nights and give you my pay check; whatever you want. Will you, Jennie?"

When I said, "Yes," he looked surprised, or was it disappointment? I could not tell. He did not seem to know what to say, so he laughed.

Finally, he asked, "May I kiss you?"

I laughed. I guess he forgot about the kiss.

"I'll bring you a ring next time I come. It won't be any little chip either. Let's tell Ophelia and Hank."

We asked them to come from Lee's down to the corner where Perry told them. Hank wished us happiness for perhaps ten minutes. Ophelia did not say a word.

112

The silence around Ophelia grew so acute that Perry turned to her and asked, "Do you mind if I marry Jennie?"

Ophelia said, "I'm sleepy," and walked away.

When I went upstairs she was in my room and for the first time she made no attempt to pretend. "Jennie, don't do it! You don't love him. It won't work. Don't let Perry ruin your life. He's the same self-important, dictatorial type as Bob. They're no good as husbands, Jennie. All they are interested in is themselves. He will make you miserable for the rest of your life."

"I thought you like Perry," I said.

"I did until I discovered there were men like Hank. Perry's O.K., but not for you, Jennie."

"You only go out for fun. You'll not marry anybody, so how do you know what is good for me?" I asked.

"You don't understand," she said.

Ophelia and Hank and Perry and I went to church on Sunday morning. Bert and Lou were so pleased to see us together — and in church. It meant something big to them. In fact, our being in church together got many of the people to speculating on what we were planning.

Later, in the cool of the evening, we were walking from Lee's to the hotel and we saw a group of children, and Perry made one last mistake. Or was he just reverting to his old self? He said, "Here come your precious children." There was derision in his voice.

The children gathered around me there on the street just as they did in the schoolroom, pushing each other, trying to touch me.

As we walked away, Perry said, "Listen, Hon, when we're married, all this Mexican stuff has to stop. Let's get that straight. In Tulsa you'll be my wife, and the Mexicans are out."

Suddenly, I knew I had to tell Juan that I was going to marry Perry. If he said O.K., then it would be. Juan kept telling me I had to marry an Anglo, and Perry was the only Anglo I knew who wanted to marry me.

I went to my room and picked up the Sunday paper. I had not taken time to look at it earlier. I took one look at the headlines and the next thing I knew, Ophelia was talking.

113

"No, she didn't just faint either. What happened to her was bigger than that."

"Yes, she did," Hilda said. "She just screamed and sort of folded up."

The doctor said, "Well, this shot will put her to sleep, and that's all she needs, a good night's rest will do it."

Ophelia said, "Hilda, go away and leave me alone with her. You go to sleep. You have to go to work early, and it doesn't matter what time I open the shop. I want to stay; she saw something in the paper. Something threw her into shock, and I want to know what it is. Please, Hilda."

She tried to talk to me, after she read the paper. "Jennie, in all my life in Chaparral I have never expressed my feelings toward the Mexicans. Actually, I feel as you do and just as strongly. But I learned long ago to be quiet and not let the racial differences bother me. They can't hurt you unless you, yourself, let them. I could be in a mental institution if I had let my mind dwell on the white and the brown. You are going to be your own undoing. If you don't get yourself in hand, you will have wrecked your life at twenty. Don't do it. Jennie, don't."

"You couldn't know how I feel about anything," I told her. "You feel nothing."

"I do know, Jennie, even though I can't prove it. You see, I was a child when the injustice of race prejudice hit me. I've had long years to accept what is and meet the race problem without expressing myself, but not without feeling."

There was no show of emotion in her face or in her eyes. Only her voice betrayed her. It seemed to betray the fact that, at some time in her life, she had had an unpleasant experience. What could it be? She was so calm, so sure and so confident.

All the next day I lay and looked at the ceiling. I had to — if I looked at anything. I could not move. The hard, ropy muscles of my shoulders were so painful I could not move. Ophelia did not leave my room except to talk with Mrs. Gonzales about cleaning it. The pain got worse. There was a tied-fast, iron-hard feeling that had my shoulders in a solid grip; a vise I could not break.

The children gathered in the alley behind the hotel and Mrs. Gonzales had to convince them that I was all right before they would go home. They sent up four oranges from the valley with a note written by Lupe: "Teasher get well. We wish to come to see you. We no can come. Goodbye. You we love. Your children. Your mamas."

This note from my children eased the tension in my shoulders more than the doctor's injection had done, but the pain stayed with me, pulling and tearing me.

Mrs. Gonzales brought the letter up the next morning. She placed the florist paper on my pink bed jacket that lay beside me, and as I opened it she said, "The pink rose go with the letter."

The letter said, "Please go to the hospital. The bills will be paid. This will be a gift from the people not from me, so accept this. It will be an expression of love and appreciation from my people who never meant to hurt you." It was not signed. I went to the hospital in Holtville, not because of the letter, but because the doctor sent me there to become relaxed. He said there was nothing wrong with me physically. I stayed forty-eight hours; hours of agony in my shoulders and a worse pain in my chest.

Ophelia was more upset at my illness than Hilda was and this was unusual. I thought Hilda would have understood my illness more than Ophelia — the nervous system. Hilda, who must remember that she had warned me, did not say anything. Even after the doctor explained my condition to me, it was difficult to understand that torn emotions could cause such physical pain. Ophelia was with me during the first day and most of the second. When I was awake, she would plead with me to not let the race question get me, that I should accept, compromise, anything, but not this. Hilda and I had hoped that she did not know what happened the night of the murder, but I was beginning to believe that she might understand.

At night, when the patients were asleep and the hospital lights were low, the Mexican sister who was my nurse, let Juan in and guarded the door. He walked in and stood by my bed. The knots in my shoulder had extended into my back and neck. He had a look of utter hopelessness on his face. He stood there with his shoulders slumping, tired and beaten.

I said, "The rose has wilted."

He sat down beside the bed and put his hand on my cheek. "Ah, Jennie, that my people should do this to you! To save you suffering is all I have wanted since the day on the street corner in Chaparral when you touched my arm. It was a light touch, like this, and I brushed your arm aside. We didn't mean for you to feel as you feel — ever, any of us. I told you the announcement of the murderer in the paper would be wrong. Why do you grieve? Don't you believe me? My people are all worried unto illness for you — and afraid. Do not grieve."

His Mexican accent was more pronounced, and I realized that in moments of stress he wanted to speak Spanish because he could express himself so much better in his native language. His phraseology is more *perfect* and stilted in English.

"No member of any race is worth what you feel now."

I began to cry.

"Don't, Jennie, don't." He moved his chair nearer. I put my hand in his hair and he took my hand in both of his. His shoulders shook with dry sobs.

I knew that what happened to me was of great concern to him. I knew that I had to leave him alone.

"I talked to the doctor," he said with a change of tone and attitude. "You can be back at school in a few days if you will only think so. The doctor said I could tell you this: your illness is not physical. The pain is real, yes, but it is from anguish. It is tension, and he said also anxiety. It is because you face a thing about which you can do nothing. I will take care of you, Jennie. I mean I wish I could take care of you."

The nurse opened the door quietly and said, "I am sorry Mr. Ortega, but the doctor said ten minutes."

He stood up and always I can see the look of utter despair on his face; in his slightly oriental eyes, completely so now, and the bitterness in his voice. As he walked out the door, he said

"I'd give everything I'll ever own if you were a Mexican girl."

I was back in the hotel reading the Sunday paper again. I knew it by heart, but I read it . . . the headlines and the write-up that had thrown me into a panic:

116

YOUNG MEXICAN BOY ADMITS KILLING

A thirteen-year-old Mexican boy has admitted he shot and killed a nineteen-year-old boy in Little Mexico . . .

It literally covered the paper, as if it were reporting a bull fight, thrust by thrust. Except that no ears were awarded. They were both bulls, born to lose, and they went into the ring one time — to meet their deaths. Pedro and the bull. They did not have a chance in Little Mexico — guilty or not guilty. If he did the shooting he should better, by far, have died the night the dance palace fell. He did not commit the murder. He could not have. Age was no protection across the little ditch. He did not do it, but he needed help, not panic. Hilda and Ophelia listened to me.

Lee said, "Gee, kid. I don't get it; you bein' so broke up over this little Mexican kid, but I am sorry you feel like that. I'm goin' with Bunk to the show, you girls want me, call me. Gee, Jennie, you look awful."

That night, the night before I went to the hospital, Pedro came to the Vidaurri — late. He came in the back way, skulking along in the shadows like a scared rabbit. It was as if he was sure he would meet his death, but he would fight to the finish. He knew he did not have a chance of clearing himself with the law, but he had to do one thing. He had to clear himself with me. I can still see him quivering like an aspen in the wind. Always I can see his eyes — quivering and darting — unusually large and black. He was thirteen years old and had been accused of murder. He looked doomed and forsaken, and, somehow, hopeless.

The timid knock had come at the door. At first, we thought it wasn't anything at all, just a faint rustle.

"Teasher, it is Pedro," he almost whispered. "I come in?" His entire body was a mass of constant, hurrying, motion. "I didn't do it. I didn't do it," he sobbed.

"We believe you did not do it. Now sit down and tell us about it," Ophelia said appearing very cool and calm.

"I didn't do it, Miss Camish. I didn't do it, Miss Gorman. Miss Smaltz, you know I didn't do it?"

He kept repeating his denial. He said they had not locked

117

him up because he was too young, that his father had charge of him. We knew this was not the real reason, the police would never have trusted Pedro's drunken father. We could only deduce that they had made this announcement in an effort to bring the guilty person in to confess.

Pedro kept pleading with us, "I sang the song in church, Miss Gorman. I am going to sing the other song when I learn it. The Bible say 'do not kill.' "

He could not see through his glasses because his eyes were wet. When he took them off he still could not see until Ophelia cleaned his glasses and washed his face. We continued to try to convince him we knew he was not guilty.

"I go now," he said. "Mees Cameesh — you never tell you come to Little Mexico, no? Mr. Ortega, he sick for you. I sorry if I say wrong."

He could speak better English but not tonight. He, too, wanted to speak his own language when the explanation was difficult.

I went back to school the following Monday. I was weak and shaken, but there. The children were glad to see me and clustered around, but they did not mention that I had been out of school.

Mrs. Gomez sent me a bag of tacos.

Mrs. Morin sent me a bouquet of zinnias with a note: "I am trying to be a better wife, now, Miss Camish. I thank you for showing me that I was wrong. We go to church every Sunday."

I realized I need not have refused to tell Juan of my visit to Mrs. Luz. Mrs. Morin had told him every word of it. She had been in Mrs. Luz' kitchen cleaning when we were having our *conversation*.

Panchito came in with a paper bag and said, "Here your dinner. Mr. Ortega say you do not go to the hotel today. You eat this because you are still tired."

Only then did I remember I had not told him I was going to marry Perry. I waited a week because I knew I would need strength and I had none.

I called him after three from the hotel asking him to meet me at three the next day at Mrs. Gomez' home. I had told Mrs.

118

Gomez that this was something she could do for me. He said he would not be there.

I said, "I have something to tell you, and never again will I ask you to see me. You must know by now that I am not going to bother you. But, this I must tell you."

"Jennie, whatever it is, we have been over it. It is always only a little more to hurt."

"No, this we have not been over," I said.

The next day seemed endless, but like all endless things it finally came to a close. At three o'clock I walked across the dusty road and up the street to the Gomez place. Juan's red Buick was in front of the house. How long he had been there, or where the family was, I did not know. He stood up when I walked in — tall, straight, defiant. His eyes were fixed on some point above my head. He stood at attention, as if I were an inspecting army officer. His eyes were wary and questioning.

"Does she have any coffee?" I asked.

"I made coffee," he said. "Mexican coffee." His look dared me to comment. He reached for the coffee pot and bent over the old, highly polishd library table and began to fill the cups that were waiting there.

"What do you want, Jennie?" he asked.

"I'm going to marry Perry."

His hand went rigid on the coffee pot handle and without a movement, without a word, he continued to pour the coffee. He poured it into the cup until it was filled, until it spilled over into the saucer, spilled onto the table dulling the polish, and spilled onto the floor in a brown spatter. He poured until the pot was empty, then he slowly straightened his body and took the pot to the kitchen. He did not return. When I followed him, I saw that he was still holding the empty coffee pot in his hand, and he was slouched onto a chair looking out the window.

"Juan, did you hear me?"

"Yes." He did not turn around.

"Say something."

"All right." He walked back to the living room and sat across the room from me. Carefully, he put the coffee pot on the floor and looked up at me. "You can't," he said.

"And, why can't I?"

119

"He's not the one for you."

"Oh? Who is?"

"I don't know, but I've told you many times. Marry in your own race. That's the only chance there is for happiness. You'll meet a nice Anglo. Don't get in a hurry. You're only twenty."

"So. What's wrong with Perry?"

"Several things — for you, that is."

"Name one."

"You're in the Baptist Church every Sunday morning. He's often in town, but he has never been to church with you."

"He went Sunday morning."

"A man will do anything once to marry a girl."

"One." I counted.

"He is not very courteous or considerate. I may not know much about Anglos, but whatever a person is, he seems to become more so after marriage."

"Two."

"He won't go to gatherings where they are not serving alcoholic beverage. Sure, you can drink coffee, if you want to, but he won't go unless there is liquor."

"Three."

"He never takes you anywhere except to Lee's to eat, or to Holtville to a night club there. It is still, for him, a place to drink."

"Four. Tell me, then. Why did you take Angelita to the same club where he takes me?"

"Because I knew you were there."

He walked to the door, opened the screen, looked up and down the street and said, "I'm going." But he didn't go.

"Is that all?"

"Yes." Then, he turned and yelled at me, and I knew that I had never before seen a Mexican angry. He was pale with rage. He jerked me out of the chair by my arms, and he was trembling as though trying to hold himself in.

"No!" he shouted, "I could go on and on but there's only one thing that really matters. He is trying to teach you to drink. You — you have no idea what life is all about, a young girl he has asked to be his wife, saying for half of Chaparral to hear, 'Go on, honey. Try a salty dog. It will do you good.' "

120

I interrupted: "It only has a little grapefruit juice, salt, ice, and gin. It's . . . "

"I know what it is!" he screamed. "Do you know what gin will do to you? Do you know what it can make you do? I do. I tried it. For four years I tried it. I know. Gin can wreck your life for all time, and I don't intend to see that happen to you. It will take me the rest of my life to live down some of the mistakes I made on gin; it won't happen to you."

"I don't intend to drink that much."

"Neither did I."

He became very quiet. "I'm going to kill him."

"You're what?"

"I've wanted to for a long time. Being a Mexican, legend has it that I would use a knife, but I'm going to kill him with a gun. Think it over, Jennie. Do you want a dead sweetheart, or would you rather be a widow. I'll kill him."

He started to leave, and I grabbed his arms and pushed him toward a chair. "You are not going anywhere yet. Here are some things for you to think over. You're going to marry in your own race. Yes, Angelita. She pleases you, you said. Fine. Are you going to then follow me around and check on my dates until you finally select an Anglo husband for me? I doubt that Angelita would approve of that. You — you . . . "

"You listen, Jennie. I'll go through it one more time. I am not going to marry Angelita. She wouldn't marry me, and I wouldn't marry her. Either of us would like to see the other one happily married. We are friends, I tell you. She has never loved anybody but her husband, and now her little boy. We are two lonely people, Jennie, and it's acceptable that we go out together. That is all. If you like, I'll have her tell . . . "

"I don't want her to tell me anything, or you either. It's none of your business . . . "

"No, Jennie. It is none of my business what you do. I know well how I will pay if I try to make it my business, but I am going to try it."

"You offer me nothing, but you try to tell me how to run my life. You explain that."

"I can't. I know, but I doubt if I can explain it. You're the only person I've ever known in my life that I wanted to protect.

121

I want to keep you just as you are. I want nothing and nobody to hurt you. I want to stand in front of you and keep the world from touching you. I want — I want to take care of you — and I know I can't."

"I'm no angel. Get that out of your head. There are lots of girls just like me."

"No. To me, you are very near to the angels."

"But that's not what I want to be. I want to be a woman, not an angel." Then, I added, "So, I'm not for use except something to look up to and lecture to and — and . . . "

"I wish I could make sense to you, Jennie. It is all so clear to me. Yes. I look up to you. No. I don't want to lecture you."

"You don't want me, but you don't want anybody else to have me."

"That is jealousy and frustration and bitterness, Jennie. And I have it all, but remember this: I have never said I did not want you. I've tried to get you to see that if we attempted a life together that it would be doomed from the beginning. I don't want anybody to hurt you, but if some man is going to, it won't be me, and it won't be Perry."

After a moment of silence, he said suddenly, "I love you so much that I sometimes think I don't want to live in the same country with you. I think I will leave. When I can sell out here, or make some arrangements about the cafe, I'm going south of the border. I'll never speak a word of English again, and I'll never again cross the Rio Grande. I've tried it and it has meant only heartbreak. Somewhere in the state of Chihuahua, there must be a cafe, or some kind of life."

"I thought you said your family lived south of Monterrey."

"They do. That's why I will go to Chihuahua. There's not one Anglo in this little town I know of there."

I said, "If you go to Chihuahua there may be an Anglo girl following you around, if you're not careful."

"How careful can I get, Jennie? I've tried everything I know."

"You haven't asked me to marry you."

"No, and I can't. Please go on and leave me alone. I pray every night for this love to leave me — this love that is stronger than love. When I see you, talk with you, watch you come to school — I fall apart inside."

122

"Juan, every time I think of you, I fall apart inside. Surely it must show outside. I wake up feeling weak and beaten every morning whether I've slept or not."

He looked at me in wonder, "And you want to marry Perry?"

"I didn't say that. I said I was *going* to marry him."

"Why?" he asked.

"They will all be gone by June. So I should stay here on my side of the ditch with you and Angelita on the other?"

"I've told you that will never be."

"Well," I said, "I'll tell you one last time and I won't tell you or bother you again. I'm going to marry Perry."

"No, you won't," he said. "I promise you I will kill him before I will see that happen."

"All right," I said. "You kill Perry, and I'll kill Angelita, and we will go to the electric chair together! Juan Ortega, one way or another, we will be together!"

TEN

EVIDENTLY
Mrs. Gomez had been waiting just outside for me. She followed
me to the car and waited until I was seated behind the steering
wheel before she spoke.

"Miss Camish," she said, "you help our children so much and
we want them to learn and you teach them. We believe you will
stay with us a whole year, with our beginners. Now, our children
want to learn; they do anything for you. We want to help. You
think of it, you tell us, we do it."

Forever I can see him sitting in the big, old, overstuffed
chair, with his shoulders shaking, and me walking blindly to
my car, from memory — I thought, but I must have said it aloud
for Mrs. Gomez replied: "Miss Camish, the way is long and
hard in marriage. I know true love, real love, when I see it. It
does not happen often. I cannot tell you. I do not know — I wish
I could say — but I do not know — walk with God, little one, and
we will pray for you and for Mr. Ortega."

I walked into the hotel lobby and ran up the worn stairs. I
tripped on the hole in the carpet and fell down the stairs and
felt nothing physically; no physical bruise could compete with
the bruise in my soul.

"If I didna know betta, I say Miss Jennie drunk," I heard
Cava say as I picked myself up and ran up the stairs again. I
burst in on Hilda, blabbering incoherently. Ophelia seemed to

124

be taking my problems harder recently than Hilda was, so I'd tell her.

When I tried to, she said, "Now wipe the mud off your face and start over, slowly."

I glanced into the mirror and saw mud on my face — streaks made by the powder of dust and the wetness of tears. When I finished telling her of my visit to Juan, she said, "How that poor guy must feel."

But I was suffering beyond anything he could ever know. Could she not see it? I went into the bathroom and tried to vomit out all my fury and grief.

When I came back into the room, she said, "Jennie, you have it all on your side. You can make the decision. To you, there's no reason why your plans can't be carried out. All you can see is that you are in love with him. If he loves you, why won't he marry you? Over a period of time, he has given you all the reasons, and they are actually what he says. It is because he loves you that he has these reasons. Can't you see it. Or, do you not want to?"

I was so completely alone. Hilda was my last hope. Not one other person thought I should have this man; only myself.

Hilda interrupted my thoughts. "If you love him as you think you do, please tell me why you intend to marry Perry?"

"I don't. I mean, I don't know. I thought it was a good idea, but now, I — Juan says that Perry is no good."

"Sure. Juan says Perry is no good. I don't know anything about Perry, but to Juan nobody would ever be any good for you. So, you can't consider that. But is what you feel for Juan fair to Perry?"

When I did not answer, she said, "During Christmas you got a stack of letters from Perry while you were sick about Pedro. He tried to talk to you. You wouldn't read his letters or answer the phone."

"I didn't know about them. Why didn't you tell me?"

"I did. We all did. You just didn't want to hear."

I called Perry at his hotel in Tulsa. He was not there but the voice that answered said, "If you want him, you start calling the

125

night clubs; try every one in Tulsa, and sooner or later you'll find him."

I found him. Through a din of noise and blur of voices he said, "Hello." Then he could not hear and he said, "Get out of the way, Sally, before I kick you out of the way. Close that door; I can't hear."

I said, "Go on with the whiskey, go on with Sally, or whatever you want. Don't come back here."

He said, "Hon, I just picked up this friend who works in my office. We worked late, and we're on the way home."

I said, "I don't want to get married, Perry. Don't come back."

He said, "Mexicans, I guess as usual. Hon, you keep on you're gonna wind up gettin' killed by one, or worse — gettin' married to one. You'll have fifty or sixty years to regret the marriage, that is, if you don't get killed first."

I said, "I'm going to hang up now, Perry."

"Wait, Hon," he said, "I found the best looking fur coat for you, that is if you . . . "

I said, "If you are cold, buy it."

Later, when I thought of it, I read his letters. They were all about how he was too busy to come to Chaparral, how he loved me and missed me, and how he was still looking for the perfect stone for my ring. I realized that he had probably never looked, but I did not mind. I had not even thought of him all during Christmas.

We were walking through the lobby, on the way to Lou's apartment, when Ophelia's purse came open and the letter fell onto the floor. She stood there and looked at it as Hank began picking up lipstick, compact and various other things that had fallen from the purse. Neither touched the letter, or looked away from it. He just stayed there, sitting on his heels on the floor beside the letter. He did not touch it. He had been told in the cave to leave it alone, and he did not know what to do. Ophelia stooped and picked it up and put it back in her purse.

She said, "Let's go sit on the veranda in the corner."

Lou brought out the big pot of coffee and the cake and put

126

them on the little rustic table. As Ophelia began to pour coffee into the big cups, the twilight turned her hair to reddish-brown. Her eyes were big and dark and unreadable. Her stark white dress was a misty blur, with only the green earrings showing sharply.

She said, "Bert and Lou were here when I came. They will remember the ranch couple who adopted a little girl, brought her here, educated her on borrowed and saved money then died, and left her all alone."

"Yes," Bert agreed, "I can still see the little tot about four years old, running around the lobby when they would come to town."

Lou said, "Sure, we remember. That was — let's see — twenty years or so ago."

That was twenty-two years ago, Lou. I am twenty-six." Without waiting for Lou to agree, Ophelia went on: "I was born Ofelia Gorman, and there the truth ends. Even my first name has an f instead of a ph.

"Who cares how you spell your name?" Falop had joined us.

Ophelia said, "I'm glad you are here, Mr. Falop. Now, I can resign my job, and if you'll just sit there until I finish talking, I'll never have to repeat this story, in or out of Chaparral."

He said, "Well, it beter be good. I got business."

"It will be good. That is, you will think it good," she assured him.

Ophelia looked at all of us, one by one, then she began.

"I am the daughter of a man whose name is Jim J. Gorman. My mother, his wife, was named Ofelia Lucia Jimenez. My father left my mother before I was born, and we never heard of him again. My mother thought to better herself by marrying an Anglo. Her idea of the good life for me was to live north-of-the-border as an Anglo. I was brought here and brought up as an Anglo and taught to hide my Mexican origin."

"Well, I'll be." started Falop.

"You will be quiet!" Hank said fiercely.

Ophelia continued, "I know only what I have heard. My grandparents had two daughters. The other daughter married a Mexican. They had a son, so I have a cousin."

127

Falop spoke again: "You mean in Mexico, way back there, Mexicans married whites?"

"That is what I mean. They still do. It was less acceptable then even than it is now, but it is still done."

"So, you're half-Mexican," he said sneeringly.

"No. I *am* Mexican, though my grandmother and my father were Anglo. You figure out the percentage, Mr. Falop, if you think it's worth while."

He began, "I don't think . . . "

"No. You don't," Hank said. "and don't interrupt her again."

People began to drift onto the corner from the lobby and the street. Hank kept trying to stay near enough to touch Ophelia, and she kept moving farther away.

"Well, that's the lie I've lived, and . . . "

Hank spoke up: "Honey, I just want to marry you and nothing . . . "

"I have not finished," she said and opened her purse and got the letter out. "I found this letter in the cave, though I had read it before. I did not want any of you to see it, so I put it into my purse. I guess having it fall out of my purse tonight was an act of God. I've been trying to get up the courage to tell this story since the day we were in the cave." She held the letter so I could read the address and watched my face. I knew she could read my emotions more than the others could.

I read:

Mr. Juan Ortega
Ortega Cafe
Little Mexico
Chaparral, Texas, USA

"It is addressed to my cousin. I learned he was my cousin by an accident that he did not plan, and one that is of no importance. The letter concerns me, too — it is also written to me."

She turned directly to me. "Jennie, I've met him often, in places far from Chaparral. I've tried to help, and I've tried to understand. I do understand. Jennie, will you stay? The rest of you leave, I've told you what I wanted you to hear. No, Hank. Don't go."

"Honey," Hank said, "I don't care."

But Ophelia wasn't listening; she was reading the letter. Sitting between us, she easily and rapidly translated the Spanish into English.

Dear Juan,

I asked you to go to Chaparral to see about Ofelia, not knowing what you would find. Maria Luz had sent the information that she was in love with an Anglo, and that was what her mother had sent her away for. This was all right, but Maria had heard the man was married. I knew Ofelia would not know you, and I thought perhaps you could help. I am glad you learned the man was not married, and I hope the new Anglo man is good and true. I hope that, if she never tells another person and if she marries this man, Ofelia will tell him the truth of her origin.

What a chain of unhappy events I started when I got married. Yet, I am not sorry. I did not think of what the future might bring to my children. I hope you will think of this. I am an old woman and have many regrets; marrying your grandfather is not one of them, though the way was often hard, it was also filled with joy and ecstasy.

I want to tell you how I married your grandfather.

Ophelia paused and said, "This is the last letter we will ever have from her. She died last week, and Juan just learned of it yesterday. I don't remember her, but his grief is very strong." She continued reading.

Perhaps my story may help you in your decision. He worked on our family ranch in the valley. When my father learned we loved each other, he gave my Juan only a few hours to get out of the state. I knew nothing of this until I found a note after he was gone telling me to marry in my own race, and that he loved me. We had been through a year of yes-and-no, such as you describe in your letter. I followed him into the black hills of Mexico (not the part that you knew). There, I walked into the little adobe house, in the little village, and I said, "Juan Jimenez, I have come. I am here. Do with me what you will. Here I stay." We were married that day, and I never heard from my family. I never again crossed the Rio Grande River. Yet, I would do it all over again.

129

Ophelia stopped and said to me: "Jennie, I almost passed out the day I met you. I've seen pictures of her at the time she married. She was tall and fair and looked so much like you I was frightened."

Nothing could keep the people away once they heard about Ophelia. They joined our group from every direction. They couldn't stay away.

"Nothing could change you, Miss Gorman," some were saying.

"We don't care if you're every bit Mexican," said another

"I guess you're the sweetest young lady anywhere."

"What would the Baptist church do without you."

No matter what you are, you're the same."

"We don't care. Just don't ever leave us."

"What you do for the Mexicans."

Everybody was talking, and they were all talking at once, until you could not hear any of them. I have never seen Ophelia so happy. She just smiled and smiled. Hank kept saying, "Marry me," and she replied, "I'm not finished."

Cava summed it up with, "I guess Miss Ophelia my color ever 'body keep lovin' her. They nobody like her. Whole town, both towns just keep on lovin' her anyhow."

Ophelia said, "I can't thank you tonight. I'll stay here and help both my people all I can. I'll try to show you, but please go now. I want Hank and Jennie to hear the letter."

Ophelia began to read again:

My son, your stormy courtship of the Anglo girl is much like my own; the attempts to not hurt each other — the longing and the times of hope and despair — the fury at the people — times of knowing it will work — times of knowing it won't. Ah, I know — I know.

Here is the way it would be: Everywhere in Anglo towns, when you came in they would say loudly, for her to hear, "That looks like a white woman with that Mexican. He is so dark." Never would you be in peace there. In Mexico they would be courteous and outwardly accept the marriage, but she would never be wholly one of them until near the end of her life. By then, she may have made it. Always, you would want to kill when her name was mentioned. Always she could hear and know. It would be hard for you, my son, yes. But the girl — I know

130

about the time of decision, the things one goes through. I wish I could tell you exactly what to do and know it was right. I cannot, but I will say some things: She is the one who will face the crowd, even though you spend your life in front of her and fight for her all of your days. She will have to love deeply, hear nothing and always be stronger in this than you. She will have to somehow rise above the disapproval, and how I cannot say.

I do not know this girl. You tell me she has no family. You are all that she will have. You will have to be very patient. Many times you will not understand each other, but you must learn to accept each other. Do not try to make her a Mexican. I hope she will be happy that you are a Mexican.

Your children will be not white, not brown. They will be a lovely coffee-with-cream color, but where will they live in happiness, and what — ah, we cannot look into the future. That, I should not mention; the next generation. I keep asking myself, "what have I started?" Since the death of your grandfather, I have had many years to think. Many things I do not know.

If you and the girl love so deeply, you know you cannot live in happiness without each other, knowing this is the way it will be, than I give you my blessing. If you can live without each other, leave there, and leave no trace behind. Never look back. Decide carefully. Remember, "until death do you part" is a very long time.

If you do decide to marry this girl I want to send you my wedding ring. She might wear it on a chain around her neck if she likes only modern jewelry, or she may put it in a drawer. But I would like this girl to have this ring. Either way, walk with God, both of you. I believe you are going to need Him every step of the way, regardless of the path you choose.

Vaya con Dios, mi hijo,

Mary Alice Jimenez

Ophelia slowly folded the letter and put it back into her purse. "See Jennie," she said touching the edge of the envelope, "Juan carried it in his pocket and read it many times. I have read it so many times that I know it from memory. I saw her so many years ago, I don't remember her. Yet, she made a better more truthful woman of me. I wish I had known her."

"I wish I had known her," I said. "Does Juan know you read this and told us this?"

"Oh, no. He did not want me to. I've talked with him about what I've just said tonight, many times, and he did not want me to. He said that my life was in order now and that I would ruin it all if I told it now. But, you can tell him about it Jennie, if you want to."

As I went up the stairs, I heard Hank say, "Honey . . ." and I smiled. I felt calm and sure. Upstairs, in private, I would call Juan. I knew now that everything would be as we wanted it.

There was no answer at the cafe. I let the phone ring and ring — into an empty building. I went over to the wavy mirror to clean my face and I saw the letter, sealed, addressed with a typewriter to me, and I knew that life was going to be wonderful. I ripped it open hurriedly.

February was a time of peace — peace and being busy and waiting, waiting patiently for the first time. Ophelia had accomplished more in one evening by telling of her Mexican blood than I had been able to do in all the months I had been here, with temper tantrums, pleadings, nervous attacks, explanations, jealous accusations, and hard work. My being an Anglo limited my effectiveness. I would continue with the children, and let come what may. Juan had left Little Mexico the night that Ophelia was telling of her past. During that same night he had, by leaving, attempted to break the very things she had cemented — a new Mexican-Anglo relationship in Chaparral. She had cemented it for herself, and it could not help but have some carry-over effect. Juan did not know of this, but he would eventually. He would return, or I would know he did not care. By announcing that Juan was her cousin, Ophelia would cause the people who accepted her to surely give him some sort of acceptance (though I knew neither of us would ever be loved as she was).

In the meantime, the people said that Miss Gorman had the biggest shower in all their memories, both in attendance and in the number and luxury of the gifts. It was given in the largest house in Chaparral, and there was not room in the house for the gifts, to say nothing of the people. There were a few Anglos who did not come; there always would be. From Little Mexico, only Mrs. Luz came, though they had all been invited. Many of them

132

gave her small gifts later. Mrs. Luz had brought a silver coffee service which was easy — coming must have been the difficult thing for her to do. I admired her a little.

Hilda and I added our set of embroidered cup towels to the array of expensive gifts. I wore my red dress, which had been cleaned, and the red shoes. Hilda wore her blue dress. Lee did not go. She thought this was "a bunch of foolishness." She and Bunk gave Ophelia a hand-drawn tablecloth they got across the river from Holtvillle.

Ophelia's wedding was in the Baptist church, which overflowed more than had the home where the shower was held. Again, all the Mexicans were invited, and also again, only Dr. and Mrs. Luz were there. Anna walked down the aisle, quietly and daintily, and while she tossed white rose petals on the carpet, Pedro sang, "I Love You Truly."

The Anglos had accepted Ophelia one hundred per cent; no, not quite. There was Falop and some of his friends and a few others. But for most of the people, Anglo and Mexican, Ophelia had not changed. They still admired, loved, and accepted her. To most of them, it was as if her birth announcement had not taken place. I suspected it would be another generation away before another girl, such as she, was accepted like this. I knew she had done it by being the kind of person she was.

Hilda continued to do good work. I determined anew to concentrate on the children — and I waited. The hard, knotted, iron-hard spots of tension I had, became areas that were sore and tender and weak. In a state of lethargy, I helped Hilda get Ophelia ready for the big wedding and the wedding trip. They left in the proverbial shower of rice after we had dressed the bride for the second time that day — the clothes for traveling.

It was not cold weather. I was now wearing my pink dress for school with Ophelia's pink sweater. Ophelia had so many new clothes she gave Hilda and me the ones we could make long enough. We were both better dressed than we had ever been. We wondered where they would go for their wedding trip. Of course, they had not said, and we just barely refrained from asking. But we did speculate on whether they would go to Mexico or to some place where they had never been. I wondered if they would see Juan. Where would he have gone? To Chihuahua, I felt sure.

That night I slept the long, peaceful sleep of youth and faith. I had been somehow cleansed of fighting and temper and grief and doubts. The soreness began to melt away.

I sat in my classroom and tried to think of new things to do. It was warm enough to play outside if we kept our sweaters on, and some of the children had already taken off their shoes. They wore them only when the weather made it necessary. That is, the ones who had shoes wore them.

Pedro smiled at me as I looked up at his jeans, his shirt, and saw the handkerchief sticking out of his pocket. It was clean and had no holes. Pedro had his shoes on still, and he had polished them to a high shine.

"Teacher," he said, " I want to write for my mother a little letter, saying how nice it is to be clean. You help me with the words, yes?"

Yes, indeed I would.

I looked out the classrom door toward the dance palace and remembered the last feast day they had made any attempt to celebrate. And then only the children celebrated, with Mrs. Gomez and Mrs. Garcia in back with the little ones. It had been September the sixteenth, Mexican Independence Day. It was a big day to them — dancing, eating, drinking, firecrackers. It was a day and a night of carnival.

This day I had gone to school and had been surprised that the children were not there. Then, I saw their multicolored dresses and the multicolored streamers of crepe paper flying from their little hands. They were coming down the narrow, twisting, rocky little path from the top of the hill. They were singing. The mothers simply brought them to the school like this, and we draped the crepe paper streamers around over the room. This was their celebration — a poor imitation of past gay times, but one of theirs had been shot, and one of theirs would be accused of it.

Chacha's scream brought me back to the present. I heard her scream, and then there were weak shrieks of fear coming from other children. Chacha had broken her arm. I don't know yet how she got up onto the roof of the bathroom during recess, but she fell off and hit a pipe on top of the ground. She was

134

too little to have climbed up there without help, but fear kept the children from talking about it.

Pedro ran all the way to the top of the hill to get Dr.Luz. He rushed madly down the hill with Pedro in his car, only to discover that he had left some necessary medical supplies at home. He called his wife and explained what she should bring.

"I don't care what you're doing, I don't care how busy you are, or how inconvenient you think it is. Tell your bridge group to drink coffee while you are away, but you get here in a hurry."

Mrs. Luz did not hurry. She drove her Cadillac up slowly, got out, and walked slowly around to the back of the classroom as if she were being admitted to a prison. The children were standing around wide-eyed, silently sympathizing with Chacha. The arm had a bad break. She lay in the sand where she had fallen. She held up the uninjured arm to me and said, "Teacher" in a hurt, puzzled, little-girl voice, just as her mother knelt on the other side. Her fear appeared to have subsided until Mrs. Luz walked up. Then she began to cry again.

"Get back, Maria," the doctor said. "She is afraid of you."

Mrs. Luz walked out slowly and did not look back. Mrs. Gomez and I stayed on the ground beside Chacha until the doctor set the arm and got it in a cast.

That night, Mrs. Luz called me at the hotel. "Miss Camish," she said, "may I come to see you at the school tomorrow after school?"

"No, we've already said it all."

"But, Miss Camish. I want to help."

"All right, in that case . . ."

I hung up. Usually I got hung up on.

She came in her Cadillac at precisely three o'clock. She seemed to be nervous, yet she was subdued.

"I have so many clothes I don't need, I was wondering if some of the mothers could use them?" she asked.

"I'm sure they could, but are you sure you want to do this?"

"Very, very sure, Miss Camish," and she looked straight into my eyes.

We unloaded the clothes from her car with Pedro's help and put them in one corner of the room. Notes to the mothers disposed of the clothes the next day. I would have loved to alter some of them for myself and for Hilda, but I knew I could not stand to do this.

Before she left, Mrs. Luz said, "Miss Camish, I have three degrees in music from various places. They are just going to waste, and I am wondering what you would think of my giving Pedro piano lessons? Miss Gorman says he has much musical talent."

"He does, but where?"

"In my home. I have my piano there. Also, he could practice there."

"But why are you doing all of this?"

As Perry used to say, "You never can leave it alone."

"I have several ideas, Miss Camish, of ways I could help my people. I mean, our . . . "

"You're changing your frame of reference aren't you? My people — our people?"

"I deserve anything you care to say to me," she said, "but please say it now so perhaps then we may work together."

"I just want to know one thing. Why did you change your mind?"

"I think my emotions got the better of me. Only, one thing did impress me. When the little child held up the arm to you, when she was afraid of me, I remembered my own daughters when they were small, and . . . " Her voice broke.

I told her nothing would make me happier than for her to help our people and that she could accomplish things I could not if I tried the rest of my life.

"No, my dear," she objected kindly, "you have practically performed miracles."

With the children, perhaps, but with Juan there had been no miracle — he was gone.

At the end of February the dance palace had been completed. We all had our names written on Chacha's cast. Pedro could sing five songs all the way through. Mrs. Luz said he had much talent on the piano. The little boys in the quartet had made much progress under Ophelia's training. Now, Mrs. Luz had taken this over also. She was teaching some of the little girls how to knit. She was doing all of this in her home. She and Dr. Luz were in the church at Holtville most Sundays, and they were taking others who did not have a car. Lucia and Paula finished skirts from material Mrs. Luz brought, on my little second-hand portable sewing machine. I had brought the machine to school for them to use, and I never did get my piece of green gingham cut out!

All the children were writing and speaking English. Dr. Luz had the Gomez car repaired. The false accusations against Pedro had not been dropped, but there had been no mention of it for some time. But I knew the murder would come up again, sooner or later.

I heard Linda say, "My mama and papa run the cafe for Mr. Ortega."

Panchito said, "Yes, but nobody allowed upstairs to clean. It is locked. Very dirty, I guess."

Mrs. Gomez called me at school: "Miss Camish, I have cook all the Mexican food you like. Please to come eat at the cafe after school. You get home before dark, I see."

As I ate, I waited. She and her husband would glance toward me and then toward each other, then back toward me. When there was no one in the cafe, they came over to the table. They said they had a worry. The man from the bank had come to see them. He told them that Mr. Ortega had more than three thousand dollars in the bank in a checking account, and they were adding to this. Mrs. Gomez said the cafe was making money and that they kept the amount agreed upon as their salary and put the other in the bank. She said the people paid for what they ate, and I should not believe they did not do this. The man from the bank had told them that if Mr. Ortega was not coming back, he should have the money in a savings account and make more money. If they would give him the address, he would write and ask Mr. Ortega about it.

The old fury hit me right in the solar plexis again. Why were they looking for Juan? Certainly, the banker did not care whether he earned any interest or not, or was it a man from the bank who had come? Only Juan could make this change at any rate.

I said, "Don't ever tell anybody where he is. Leave his money just as it is. If anyone else comes to see you tell him nothing."

"We don't know where he is. If you want we give you the bank slips to mail to him so he know we do what he say."

"Neither do I know where he is." They looked as though they did not believe it.

Then Mr. Gomez said, "He will return. He cannot stay away. This I know. I will find him if . . ."

"No," I said, "leave him alone."

Ophelia and Hank returned in March. They had spent the first night of their marriage in the cave and had gone on to visit her mother. They had not seen Juan's mother, but they had learned that he had not been there. They stayed at the hotel about half the time now, going out to the ranch when necessary.

One day Ophelia said, "Jennie, if I had only told I was Mexican when Juan first came here, I could have saved so much trouble and sorrow. I don't know why I didn't. When he first told me about you, I offered to, and he told me to go ahead and get my own life straightened out, that he would take care of his. Ah, Jennie, if I had only known how it would all be. You've tried so hard, and I've done so much hurt instead of giving help. Juan was deadset against my telling it, but that's only an excuse. I should have done it long ago. I think I've wanted to since I can remember. Always I've felt the lie inside of me.

"I didn't expect happiness for myself when I told it. Please, believe me. I thought you'd call him and tell him, and it would all be settled between you. I hoped it would pave the way for both of you, but I didn't think it would get me Hank."

"It would have," I said, "if he hadn't just happened to leave that same night."

"Jennie, he will be back," she said.

"I know he will," I replied.

"Jennie, you are so sure. Where is he? What do you hear from him?"

"I don't know where he is. I don't hear from him. I just know he will be back."

"Sure, Jennie," she said, "we will find him. I mean Hank can find him. But, Juan may be furious with me, at first."

138

I said, "No, he is taking care of his own life as he told you he would. Just leave him alone, Ophelia."

All the people who had ever tried to keep me away from Juan were now offering to find him for me. Life is very strange, some of the time.

"Ophelia," I said, "you've known the whole story all along, haven't you?"

"Yes," she replied, "from the day of the ham sandwich, so I, too, know he will be back."

It was nearing the end of March, and Carl was expected the following week, so we gave Hilda the shower in Bert and Lou's apartment. It overflowed, too. Close friends from Chaparral and from her office in Holtville came. It was not such a shower as Ophelia's had been; there would never be another shower like that, but this one was nice, small and intimate.

During the shower Hilda was called to the telephone. Cava said, "It's from that place down in South America."

I remember how pretty and happy she looked. I had been watching her as she sat in front of the tea service. She had been sitting on a low hassock, with her full, blue skirt spread around her on the floor like an open umbrella. Her carrot hair and her carrot freckles and her reddish eyes were gleaming with love and happiness. We waited and waited but she did not return to the shower.

ELEVEN

HILDA
was sitting in my room on the bed, looking at the floor. The light had gone out of her eyes. She was staring, just staring at the floor. She did not look up when we came in. Her body was hunched over in an attitude of black despair, her hair looked dull, tousled and uncombed. She still had on her shoes. We always took our shoes off when we came into the room.

I said, "Hilda," as I put my hand on her shoulder. But, there was no response. None at all. She was tightly holding the envelope; the yellow paper with the telegram on it lay on the floor. She kept staring at it, staring as though she did not believe it. I saw that it was signed by the superintendent of the oil company in South America where Carl worked. It said that Carl had been killed in a drilling accident that day and that the sender regretted having to deliver such tidings. That was all it said.

Hilda died that day. True, she went on breathing, but the life went out of her walk and her talk and her hair and her eyes. Her body took on a slump that she never completely lost. All signs of animation left her. Lee, Ophelia, and I tried to talk to her; but she did not hear us. She did not hear anything we said. The doctor gave her a shot to relax her. It did not. All night long she sat and stared.

If she could only cry — or scream — or anything.

A party to announce a wedding should be the happiest time

140

of a girl's life; her's was one of the saddest. It took Hilda a week to cry and a week to stop crying. The shock and grief poured of her in torrents, day and night — night and day.

During the time of her grief she looked as though she had no mind, and all the time she was making a major decision that she was to tell us about only a couple of weeks later. Something new was taking the place of old Hilda. The suffering was buying her a new kind of courage. Once, just before we left the Vidaurri, she said, "I could, maybe, help people like Juan," and you could see that she was trying desperately to find a place for herself. When you have lost your place in life, you feel all lost inside, and you keep on searching for a niche in which you can make yourself fit.

Ophelia and Hank stayed at the Vidaurri the following months as Hilda seemed to fall apart. I remembered that this was exactly what she had warned me not to do. Ophelia, Lee and I spent much time with her as we could. We got her back to work, and one day she said, "I want to be a social worker. I need more education. I can get that gradually, but I'm going to stay right here, and maybe I can do some good here."

After that she began to get a little better.

Were we all going to fall apart? Each of us — the four of us — had, at one time or another. Lee had pulled herself together as a better person than she had ever been. She married Bunk in Holtville with Ophelia and Hank as witnesses and came back to work the night shift; Bunk drank coffee.

Hilda and I went to the cafe to see them just in time to overhear Falop say to a newcomer: "You can't tell me nothin' 'bout Mexicans," he laughed. "I'll remember this as the year that all the single white people in town was tryin' to marry 'em a Mexican, and . . ."

"You shut up. Don't ever say anything about Mexicans in my place of business," shouted Lee.

Falop was shocked. "Well, now," he said, "not so long ago, you said . . ."

Bunk stood up with clenched fists and Lee, without looking at her new husband, said, "Sit down, Bunk. I'll handle this."

Bunk remained standing.

"Yes, Falop," she said, "not so long ago I was as blind as you.

141

But I've changed, see? No matter what race you are, it's the kind o' person you are that counts. You show me somebody nicer'n Ophelia Gorman — I mean Holt, that is — and I'll eat your hat."

"So," Hilda said smiling at me, "we scored again."

We were back in the corner of the veranda: Ophelia, Hank, Lee, Bunk and Hilda and I. The pale light of the street lamp was shining on Lee's light brown hair.

Bunk said, "Your hair is sure a pretty color, Baby," as if they were alone.

Lee said, "Now, you all just listen a minute. I got somethin' I wanta tell, too. I taught myself to hate Mexicans, and I drank gin to make the hating easier. I married one, see? He wasn't so much Mexican, and it wasn't so much of a marriage. I stayed black from his beatings; and when I had a baby, he left. He had just a little bit o' Mexican blood from 'way back there somewhere, but almost none." She looked tenderly at her husband. "Bunk, here, taught me that there's good in every race; don't matter what kind o' blood you got. It's what you do 'bout the blood. I never did like the taste o' that durn gin anyhow. My boy . . . "

Bunk interrupted her, "He's eight. We're goin' after him next week. I want to — "

"And," Lee broke in, "I'm going to spend the rest of my life teaching him to be proud he's a Mexican and proud he's an Anglo."

Ophelia kissed her cheek and that, somehow, spoke for all of us.

"You'll come back here, won't you?" asked the ever-sensible Hilda.

"Yes," replied Bunk, "she wants to keep on at the cafe. I got plenty of work here for a while. We want us a house, and she says we can get it quicker that way."

Hilda was not over Carl's death; she never would be. But she continued to work and to plan, and we helped her. We walked in the park where the zinnias were getting ready to bloom once more. Buds were ready to pop out all over the hills and in people's yards. Hilda, at Mrs. Luz' invitation, was working with

142

her, trying to learn the needs of the individual Mexicans in Little Mexico. Hilda told me later they had started by trying to get Mrs. Garcia to take a bath, but that it was late summer before they were able to get this done. After that, Mrs. Garcia not only kept herself and her family clean, she cleaned her house — once. Mr. Garcia stayed sober part of the time the following summer.

It was March when Mrs. Luz once again called to invite me to her home. When I refused, she asked if she might come to the school. She came, and we talked about the children for a while, and then she asked me where Juan was.

Until then I had thought my bitterness toward her was over, but it rose up again.

"I don't know, Mrs. Luz. I told you that you would have no control over my life once, but you did, you know. I met Juan Ortega here at the school the night I was at your house. I told him nothing of the conversation, but I did exactly as you would have me do, Mrs. Luz. I didn't know that I would, but I did. I started that night the process of stopping whatever relationship there was between Juan and me. I'll never tell you what it was, Mrs. Luz. It worked for you; you told me that once, too. You do good work for your people. Miss Smaltz says you are really helping them. Your people need you. I think they need me, too. As I told you once before, also, I intend to stay here.

"You had just what you wanted of me. You told me to leave Juan Ortega alone. Now, Mrs. Luz, you leave him alone. I hope you are happy, but never mention his name to me again!"

"I am very unhappy," she said. "Both my husband and I. We deeply regret — I deeply regret — I regret . . . what can I do?"

"Just leave me alone."

"Miss Camish, I know the relationship — what it was, and is — between you and Juan. Juan told me before he left, and again the night he left, how he feels toward you. Ophelia showed me the last letter Mary Alice Jimenez wrote to Juan; so I know." She smiled sorrowfully. "The things you said to me are nothing compared to the bitter words Ophelia used, and I think Juan would have killed me had I been a man. Juan will return. This he cannot prevent. He doesn't know of Ophelia's marriage. If he knew — we can locate him, my dear — would you like . . . ?"

143

"NO! LEAVE JUAN ORTEGA ALONE."

I went home that night and read the letter again, the one that Mrs. Gonzales had left in the wavy mirror that night Juan left. I had gone upstairs after Ophelia had talked to us in the corner of the veranda. I had long ago memorized it. I kept it in my purse. No one else had seen it. It was mine alone. It was creased and smudged, but it gave me all the courage I had; of all the people trying to find Juan for me, none of it helped. This was not the way to do it. Only the letter kept me going to work and holding in my tensions, and only the letter gave me the little courage that I had.

I read, "I am going somewhere south of the border. Do not feel to blame. I am running away from myself only. I can no longer stay here, knowing that I only upset you. Please believe that none of it is your fault.

"I suppose Perry is all right. I believe it is that I am jealous. I think the sooner you marry an Anglo — Perry if you want — the happier you will be — the more at peace you will be.

"When the Rio Grande has filled in with dirt, and is level with its banks, from Colorado to the Gulf of Mexico, when there is no river to cross — then, will we meet again."

. . . Teasher, We Gather the River . . . the golden river that
flows by the throne of God . . .
We shall gather at the river,
The beautiful, beautiful river,
Gather with the Saints at the River,
That flows by the throne of God.
. . . No! I did not believe that he would wait that long to
meet me again.

In April, spring arrived in Chaparral. The redbud trees, popularly called the "Judas tree" in our area, were walking down the side of the hills in an uneven, staggering line, dots of purplish-red. The Judas tree we would not see by the Golden River. The sand was hot, and the days were bright. We gave Lee her wedding gifts as she sat in the veranda corner. Hilda and I gave our hand-embroidered tea towels. Ophelia gave her an oak bridge table with four matching chairs, something she

144

had heard Lee say she would like to have for snacks in her hotel room.

Mrs. Luz sent Lee a silver coffee service, similar to the one she had given both Ophelia and Hilda. Since she had met neither Lee or Bunk, we deduced that some of Lee's more recent comments regarding the Mexicans had filtered into Little Mexico. I knew, somehow, that Mrs. Luz would always send a silver coffee service as an approval gift to any Mexican-Anglo marriage shower, or to any couple who had spoken up in defense of the Mexicans.

April first was my birthday. I never thought it would be exciting. It only made me twenty-one. But I had a surprise birthday party at school. Mrs. Morin brought the punch. Mrs. Gomez brought the cake. The little girls served in paper cups and plates. After they had gone, Pedro gave me an extremely mongrel dog which had not eaten recently but who had a multitude of fleas. He said, "I bring you a present," and ran. I named the dog Redbud — for the day — and Mrs. Gomez kept him at night, and we kept him at school during the day.

As I sat with Redbud in my lap — collecting fleas — I saw that the dance palace was almost finished. I remembered the last time the people had made any effort to celebrate a feast day — September Sixteenth, the Mexican Independence Day. I knew that in the past, there had been dancing, eating, drinking, games, firecrackers, and a total carnival atmosphere for the day and night on September Sixteenth. This day I had seen them coming, winding along the crooked, dusty, narrow path, down the hill, in single file. All of the children of Little Mexico, and only Mrs. Gomez and Mrs. Garcia were at the back of the line guiding the little ones.

They were a long splash of many colors, with their Mexican dresses and the crepe paper streamers. How these people loved a fiesta! They are, essentially, a happy people, the Mexicans. But they had an unsolved murder hanging over their heads. So, only the children were gay. They came down the hill singing, waving the streamers and came to school. We draped the streamers around the room and that was their only celebration. I knew that eventually the murder had to be pinned on somebody, or perhaps even solved, so that they might go back to being the kind of people they really were.

The men were talking more and more about what was happening in the war in Europe, but we seldom even looked at the paper. I noticed the absence of the newspaper rack in the lobby, so I asked for a paper.

"Cava, where is the paper rack?"

"Well, Miss Jennie, it wuz right heah. I declah . . . " He looked all around ostensibly trying to locate it.

"Cava, where is the paper rack?" I repeated.

"Well, you see, now, it was right . . . "

"I know it was right there, but where is it now?"

" 'Jes' a minit," he said as he picked up the phone.

Lee and Bunk came in. "Come on, kid," Lee said, "let's go upstairs."

Ophelia, Hank, Hilda were in my room when we went in. They all looked at me as if they had a death message for me.

"Come on, tell me what it is," I demanded. "Somebody is always trying to keep something from me."

"O. K., Jennie," Ophelia said and resignedly handed me the paper.

I read the headline and I became a mass of ice — cold, wet, slippery, with my heart pounding so fast I could not breathe. There was no air in the room. The breath was being squeezed out of me by the band of ice. It was heavy and cold, a band I could not break. It was the same, and somehow different from the time Pedro had been falsely accused. I wondered if they would really condemn an innocent man, then, or just make him suffer for a long, endless time. After some hot milk and many blankets, and when I could see, I read the article in detail:

LOCAL MEXICAN ARRESTED FOR MURDER!

The article retold in detail the story of the murder. It said that the police had known, since the beginning, that Juan Ortega was the murderer; they were only waiting for him to make a move. He had made it, under cover of darkness he had slipped out; he had returned in darkness. It was known that criminal always

146

returns to the scene of the crime, that he was under the influence of alcohol and that he was extremely dangerous. The brave officers of the law had overpowered this dangerous drunk and had him in Holtville in jail, that the people were safe now from the maniacal killer.

I felt the knots of tension pulling and getting harder. I felt, also, the need to do something now.

"I'm going to Holtville."

"It's too late, Jennie. Tomorrow is Saturday, and some of us can go over in the morning," Hilda said.

Hank said, "No, Jennie. You stay out of it. We have been over there. He doesn't want you there."

Ophelia told me he had refused to see them until they had found the chief and had his cell door unlocked anyway. She said he asked her to see that I did not come to the jail, that he had not resisted the arrest, that he had not been drinking, but had been fatigued from driving night and day, that he would never have left if he had thought they wanted to see him, that they had broken in the door to his apartment just after he got in and before he had time to unlock the door. He told her he had not gone to Chihuahua, nor had he gone to his mother's. He had gone beyond any of the places he knew to an Indian village, where there were no Anglos, no English, and no modern customs.

Ophelia said, "Jennie, Hank got him the best lawyer in the county. He will be out of there in no time. He's done nothing wrong. Wait a few days, Jennie, and he will come to you."

Saturday morning I left Chaparral right after breakfast. As I walked through Lee's on my way out, I listened to odd bits of conversation.

"Goin' to Holtville to see that Mexican killer," I heard Falop say.

Lee said, "Leave her alone. You can't stop her, her feelin' like she does. Now, you shut up!"

Ophelia said, "If you'd only wait. I don't want you to see him like this."

Hank walked to the car with me. "Jennie, we will all, or any one of us, go with you if you want."

"No," I said, "I have to go alone."

147

"Yeah," he said, "I guess you do."

The road to Holtville was long. Always before, it had been short. But today it had no end. The skies were dark and cloudy, and the air was cool and soft, and driving should have been heavenly if I could have only felt or seen it. It should have been a lovely day, but it was not.

I drove alone with the river weaving in and out beside me. There it would be, and there it would not be. I would lose it for whole minutes at a time, but it would always be there, inside me and surrounding me. Sometimes I could see both sides at once. In some places it looked placid and calm and peaceful. Then, the next curve would show a muddy, brown puddle gushing over rocks. The river had many faces — ugly, dirty, sweet, clean, and bitter.

This is such a human river. It is not like other rivers. It does something to you like the music and the dance. It does to me. This side is America, and that side is Mexico, and somewhere in between there is a vast conglamoration that is neither Mexico nor America, the third side, quarter-Mexican, three-quarter Mexican, Mexican haters, American haters. People who defend Mexico are called Mexican lovers. I guess the ones who intermarry, land right smack dab in the middle. They do not belong on either side.

Holtville looked quiet and peaceful, drowsing down there in the little valley, unaware of the fact that an innocent man was wasting his time in jail. Or, did Holtville care? Holtville was on this side of the river.

I had no difficulty in finding the jail. It was the oldest building there. What it may once have been, I had no idea. It reminded me of the Alamo, except that it was perfectly flat on top. It had thick adobe walls burned to dust color by many hot summer suns. It was a long, narrow, no-color monstrosity, and it smelled — like a jail.

I had parked across the street and watched the officers of the law — the body that enforces the rights and protects the innocent. They were rocking in the sun — two of them, rocking with their feet on the porch railing — and *Mexico* was supposed to be the land of mañana!

As I walked up the steps, trying to miss the tobacco juice,

the men stopped rocking. They both stopped in unison. They neither moved nor pulled their Stetsons from over their eyes, but I felt their eyes appraising me. I began to wonder what one was supposed to wear when calling on a guest of the jail; what clothing would not slide off as you were being appraised? I had on my red dress when I left the hotel, now I felt completely naked! I looked down; I still had it on.

One of the men said to the other, low and secretive, "Bet that's that girl come to see the Meskin. "Chief said let 'er see 'im, but not by herself."

"She looks decent-like."

Never had I wanted to turn and run and get into my car and break even Perry's record for fast driving. I wanted to go home, home to the Vidaurri. I almost did, but I knew I had to do this, to say this, the things for which I had come. The men would be sitting there when I came out, discussing me, but I had to go through with it. I had to try — for Juan.

. . . I'm caught right in the middle of the river and I've got to sink or swim . . . and, I'm swimming toward the Mexican side . . . Well, I will swim, and I won't look back; it is a cinch nobody here is going to extend a helping hand . . . It is icy here . . . only thing to do is plunge right in . . .

"I'm Miss Camish. Could I see the Chief?"

"What ye want?"

Thus far, neither of them had moved. Slowly, hating to leave the support of the railing, he removed his feet, pushed back his hat — onto the back of his head, and finally, stood up. "Follow me," he said.

He preceded me into a small cubicle that smelled of tobacco juice, stale cigars, whiskey and urine. He referred to this, fondly, as the office. He seated himself in the swivel chair and resumed his position while on the porch. "Now, what ye want?"

"You have a man here awaiting trial for murder, and he did not do it. He didn't murder anybody, and I can prove it."

"You're mistook, lady. We ain't got no man here accused o' murder. We got a Meskin here shot a feller in Little Mexico an' tha's all we got here. Ain't got nothin' else."

I could see he would make it difficult for me if he could, and he could.

"That's the one, I think. What's his name?"

"I dunno. Organ, or somethin' like that. I don't never pay no 'tention to them Meskin names; all sound alike."

"It's Juan Ortega, and he's innocent, I tell you. innocent."

"Well, now, young lady. What makes you say that?"

"I say it because I know. I — I — well, I spent the night with him that night. I mean, I stayed all night in his apartment."

The officer was not impressed, just mildly curious. "You know, that's a awful bad thing to say 'bout yourself," he said, "that you spent the night with a Meskin. Awful bad thing."

"I didn't say that. I said — uh . . . "

"Well, just what did you say, then? Maybe I don't hear good."

"I spent the night in his apartment. My ankle was sprained and I fell, and . . . "

"I've heard a lot about them Meskins, but never heard of one of 'em hurtin' a woman's *ankle*. Hee! Hee!"

The man was exceedingly proud of his wit. I could imagine him telling the other man how funny he had been.

He asked me if anyone else had been there. I would not involve Hilda, so I answered, "No."

"Well, now, I'll tell ye. A Meskin doctor from Little Mexico come over and said he was there. Didn't say nothin' 'bout no sprained ankle. Said he was a friend o' this here feller we got here. Guess he must not a stayed all night, huh?"

"Oh, no, he just bandaged my ankle."

"He didn't tell it that way. He said he stayed all night with this here Organ feller. You see ye did tell me somethin'."

I did not know what he meant, so I asked him.

"I mean, lady, that I don't believe a word you been sayin', and I'll tell you why. The law has its way. That doctor *he* didn't know about no woman bein' there. That Organ he didn't say nothin' 'bout no woman, and if they can lay it onto somebody else they're a goin' to. Furthermore, ain't no American girl, 'specially no school teacher, gonna go stay all night with no Meskin. You'd a done that, they'd a run you out o' town the next mornin', and Chaparral would o' knowed it. The police force over there is on the ball. Nothing like that will get by them. No, siree, it's

150

not possible. Why you're doin' all this I dunno, but I aim to find out. Now, go on back to Chaparral, and keep ye mouth shut. No, girl, they's not a word of truth in anything you say. Now, listen to me. Go on home and don't open your mouth about these crazy ideas you have."

. . . Hilda, you told me nobody would believe me . . .

I learned later that this man was not the police chief, nor was he even the lowest ranking man on the force. In fact, he was not on the police force. He was sitting-in while the sergeant went to get a cup of coffee! He was having a heyday out of my visit. He would tell it for years, with relish.

"You don't mean you want to see that Meskin killer?" he protested when I became insistent.

"I do."

"Why?"

"He is a friend of mine."

"All right, you got no more sense 'n that, but I warn ye, don't try nothin', don't give him nothin'. Come on. I'll give ye five minutes, but I won't take my eyes off you; so be careful; be real careful. Now, I'll protect you, he tries anything, but don't get too close to him. He's dangerous. A dangerous criminal; that's what he is."

. . . Juan — Juan, so sweet and gentle and not wanting to hurt . . .

Juan blinked in the faint light. It seemed to take forever for him to recognize me standing right in front of him. Even after he knew me, he looked as if he did not believe it, as if he did not want to believe it.

"I told the man all about that night, and he didn't believe it. He didn't believe a word of it!" I blurted out, not realizing that this was exactly what Hilda had told me long ago — long ago.

"Why? What do you know to tell the man? Nothing!"

"Why? Because you're innocent and it's got to be proved. Somehow, it just has to be."

He made a faint gesture; a Latin shrug. He didn't do any-

151

thing. He only said, "Now, go. Please go, and don't come here again. You have no business here."

"You mean you're willing to die for something you didn't do? For something I know you couldn't have done?"

"No. But they'll discover who did it before it's over."

"And, if they don't?"

He smiled sadly, an age-old, resigned smile. He smiled a Mexican smile, not three-quarter, or half-breed, just an all Mexican smile. And I knew then that he was glad he was a Mexican, and he must have known that nothing would ever change him. *I* knew it.

"Time's up," the guard said.

As I left I looked back at Juan; he was looking completely alone, completely shocked, unshaven and bitter.

All the way home the sides of the river kept pulling toward each other, trying to meet, straining and pushing, getting closer and closer, but they could not quite make it to the middle. If they could only get together, there would be no river, no river to cross. Both sides would be the same, both sides and the middle. I would see a wide expanse of dry land and then I would see the river getting wider and wider until it was coming right into my car. I have to get hold of myself, I kept telling myself, but nothing happened.

The shrill whistle came in at the window, and I was almost pushed off the road. Pushed into the river, the river, the river, The river had gone — just gone.

"Lady, do you know you're doing ninety? The speed limit is seventy. You'll get yourself killed. What if a car had come around that hill?"

The highway patrolman peered at me closely and said, "Is this an emergency?"

I can understand why he asked that now. I must have looked as if I were rushing to a death bed.

"One never does. I mean, no cars ever come along here. Just once in a while and that's usually us. No." I knew my explanation was weak, there must be a better reason. "I've been to jail. I went to see a friend," I added.

"So, you're the one. I heard about you. Well, cut her back to seventy and go on to the Vidaurri."

152

The river was still and quiet, and very dark-oily looking. The low, dark clouds were rolling slowly, just above the river, boiling, deciding, and menacing.

Hilda and Ophelia met me at the door. "We've been worried sick. Why did you go?"

Between sobs and snubbings, I told Hilda and Ophelia what I had done. Ophelia put me to bed and kept threatening to call the doctor. She said I'd make myself sick again crying like this. She said I was hysterical and must sleep.

Lee came in saying, "The Vidaurri is buzzing like a bee-hive. You'd think you'd gone to jail to commit murder yourself. What a bunch of lousy, narrow-minded idiots!" Lee was furious, all right.

Ophelia said, "I'm glad you got in. The radio says it's going to rain. Nobody believes it, but that's what the radio keeps telling us. We're going to do something. Hank is furious at the way that man at the jail talked to you. He told them they'd have to change the name of the town if they didn't let Juan out. You know, Holtville was named for Hank's grandfather. He told them I was Mexican, too, but they didn't believe it."

"That river is different," I said. "I never realized it until today, but there's nothing else in all the world like it — nothing. I know, I have never seen a real river, but that's not what I mean. This one is a — a live river. You should have been with me today, Ophelia. I bet you never saw the river in your whole life. The policeman came walking right out of the middle of it — the very center. You never saw the Rio Grande, did you, Ophelia?"

Hilda said, "Ophelia you look so white, and so sort of — strange. Don't pay any attention to her. She's emotionally worn out. She can't help talking that way, can't keep taking the things that keep happening."

TWELVE

PLAYING
on the radio was "Be Honest With Me," and all my life I would
be honest with Juan. I would be honest with any one, but why
would no one be honest with me?

It was raining outside my window. The big drops were
popping like pebbles on the window glass — so loud and so big I
thought they might break the glass.

. . . . . *I will go back over there and I will find the chief of
police* . . . . . *I will tell him the whole story* . . . . . *I will demand
that he check my story* . . . . . *I will not leave until he does* . . . . .
somehow, I will get Juan out of jail . . . . . *tomorrow, I will* . . . . .
tomorrow . . . . .

Nobody was talking about Juan. I had noticed it was much
better in the Vidaurri when they were running a Mexican down,
or something to do with a Mexican issue. They did not say
anything to me, just nothing at all. They ignored me. Of all
the efforts, of various types that I had made to get people to
leave it alone, now I did not know what to do when the subject
was completely dropped; no Mexican was mentioned in the hotel.

Sleep helps. I guess I slept. I felt that I had been drugged when
I awakened again. Nothing healed my pain. I was sore all over
and ached in all my joints, and my muscles kept tensing at the
oddest times. I would think that I had everything under control,
then I would feel the tension grabbing at me, all over, all at one

154

time, and I could not stop it. My whole life was — all inside — filling up with time, more time and a heartache — a never-ending ache that throbbed and pounded, and nothing would dull the ache.

I had passed the point of caring that I had made a fool of myself. I kept telling myself that I did not care so often, that I began to believe it. I would wake up in the middle of the night, cold, wet, hearing the man from Holtville talking — sneeringly, menacingly. I would see him, but there would be hundreds of him coming toward me, pushing their Stetsons onto the backs of their heads and saying, "He's dangerous."

Hilda had been called to Holtville early after lunch. Ophelia and Hank had gone. Lee took off from work and she and Bunk sat in my room and talked to me. The rain gradually got heavier and faster; it became darker and darker all Saturday. It was almost as dark as night, a black night. Heavy thunder rolled and dark balls of clouds rolled and grumbled.

"What a blessing for the cow ranches!" exclaimed Lee.

Yes, I thought, for the ranchers and for Lee. It will make Lee's business better, this rain.

Hilda came in after dark, breathless, white and visibly shaken. She had been in Holtville all day. The doctor had called her to come and hear Toolie's fantastic story. He wanted to listen in and see if Toolie would change any of the story.

The doctor had said to Hilda, "It's utterly fantastic, Miss Smaltz. Well — you listen to it. She wants to tell you, so we will hear it one more time. This time, use your own judgment about asking questions; say anything you think best. Our judgment may not have been so good."

Toolie was glad to see Hilda because, she said, Hilda would believe her; that the others had not.

Toolie said, "It is so simple. I wonder why they keep accusing Mexicans. I had every right to kill him, and so I did."

Hilda asked, "Kill who, Toolie?"

"Why, my husband, of course. I told you I was going to. I had his little gun. I had buried it in a box in the zinnia bed. Po gave me this outfit of clothing one time when we did the jarabe at a Lion's Club show." Toolie laughed.

155

"Where did you do the jarabe?" Hilda asked.

"Why, in my home town. Will you listen now?" Toolie was angry, then she added, "It's really the jarabe Tapatío. Some people call it the Mexican Hat Dance if they don't know any better. You know, Hilda, this is a very nice little hotel. The doors are locked at night to keep people out, but I've always known where they keep the keys. I put on these clothes. I got the gun. I got the bus to Chaparral. I . . . "

"Why did you take the bus to Chaparral?"

"Why, to kill Po, of course. I knew they did the jarabe at all Mexican places, and Po loved it, so he'd be where there was dancing."

"How did you know he would be there?"

"I can't tell you, but I had a feeling. I just knew." Toolie paused then continued, "I got off the bus in Chaparral and walked to Little Mexico. See? Here's the scar on my knee from the fall. I fell in a little ditch between Little Mexico and Chaparral."

"Weren't you afraid somebody would recognize you?" Hilda asked.

"Oh, no. I looked like any other Mexican. I stayed in the dark. You know they have their husbands or their mothers with them. Girls don't go out unescorted over there at night."

How well Hilda and I knew. We looked at each other in agreement.

"So," Toolie continued, "I didn't let myself be seen. I saw him, as I had known I would. He was dancing with a Mexican girl. His back was toward me and — "

"How did you know he was Po if you couldn't see his face?"

"Eight years and five kids and I don't know my own husband from the back? You should get married, Hilda; you'd learn a lot. You just know; that's all."

"Then, did you shoot him?" asked Hilda.

"Not right then. I watched him move across the floor until he was near the edge of the platform. I was on the ground about three feet away from him. It was a perfect shot. The next thing I knew the whole dance floor was falling toward me. I never heard so much noise. I ran. I shot and I ran. I ran in the wrong direction at first. I decided to bury the gun."

156

"Where did you bury the gun?" asked Hilda.

"Well, Miss Smaltz, you wouldn't believe it but you go over there some time and see. There is a little country schoolhouse in Little Mexico; the one-room kind they don't use any more. I buried it in the yard. It was easy to dig soft sand."

"Then what did you do, Toolie?"

"I ran back to Chaparral as fast as I could, but there was no bus, so I started walking. A Mexican couple with even more children than I have picked me up. They were in a truck. I told them all about it, but I guess they couldn't understand English. I had them let me out at the hotel."

 . . . . . *Hilda, my sweet, now I know that Juan will be free. But, you are the one who warned me about falling apart . . . . . can you hold together with this added to Carl's death? If you could only cry. I think, if not, you may fall apart now . . . . .*

"Lie down, Hilda, sleep here. I'll stay beside you."

"There is more," she said. "The doctor called me out just then and took me to his office. There, he asked if any of her story was true?"

"First," I said, "may I ask a question?"

"I will tell you anything I know, Miss Smaltz."

"Where is her husband?"

"He is dead, Miss Smaltz. He lost control of his car on a lonely stretch of road just after his last visit here. He was sleepy and upset, I suppose."

"You didn't tell her?" asked Hilda.

The doctor stood up and walked away from his desk and looked out the window. After a time, he turned to face Hilda. "In this business we do not always know what is the best. The staff discussed telling her many times. The couple had been so devoted that we were afraid she would go into the world of make-believe, permanently. We were constantly remaking the decision; each time she would have a relapse. We were wrong — I was wrong."

"Is her name Toolie?" asked Hilda.

"No, it's Alma. She has a brother. I think that I will not tell you the last name of either. That is his decision."

"That is *not* his decision!" I yelled. "This is one time the

157

decision will be made *for* Bob. No man can be a big shot forever."

"The doctor asked me again, Jennie, if any of it is true, and I told him every word of it is down to the very last detail. Forgive me, Jennie, but I told him about that night, every single word of it down to the last detail."

She slept then. I felt a peculiar sort of calm, sitting beside her. It rained harder and harder all Saturday night, on Sunday you could not see the road anywhere. The water was a solid sheet, but the cars were still moving slowly. The voices on the radio were telling us to stay off the roads unless travel was necessary and to drive with caution. It had been a steady, hard rain, and Sunday night it hit with an unleashed fury none of us in the cow ranch country had ever seen. It was frightening to hear and frightening to see. We stayed in the room and hoped Ophelia and Hank had made it to the ranch, or wherever they had gone.

Late in the night on Saturday, Hilda woke and said, "Jennie, I stayed in Holtville until Toolie's story was checked. It checked through in detail. The police found the people with whom Toolie had ridden back to Holtville. Yes, they had understood what she said. They had not gone to the police because they were afraid. They were more afraid when they read the story about the murder, and they only talked among themselves. They were afraid of the law and afraid they would have to go to court. Yes, they could see they had done wrong, but they had been, oh, so afraid. They would have gone to the jail when they they put the Mexican man there, but they heard how the police had talked to the American girl who had gone there, and they were very much more afraid.

"The bus driver remembered the girl. They found the gun in the children's sand pile! Buried not too deep, and the children had played there daily! God had been with us. The gun was ready to fire again."

Ophelia and Hank came in about ten o'clock on Sunday morning. Brother Way had announced there would be no church services. Nothing in town was open, the mail, the paper — nothing came into Chaparral. All roads leading out of there were closed, and the town was under martial law. We could not even go onto the veranda. The water was rolling across it in heavy swirls. The world was a solid sheet of water. Debris was

158

floating around in the street, and all the men in the Vidaurri spent Sunday trying to keep the water out of the lobby. People stayed where they were — wherever that might be. Nobody could move. The electricity went off. The water diminished to a cold trickle. The telephones went out of order. There was little to eat, and we were hungry and wanted coffee, lots of coffee. None of us had slept; we were cold.

Ophelia and Hank had come into my room at ten, but they had come in from Holtville the night before, just before the road was closed to traffic. They thought Hilda and I were asleep, so they did not disturb us.

Yes, they knew the entire story of Toolie. Juan had been released, theoretically, but he was waiting in the jail until Monday, to go through the red tape. He had been moved to a clean room in the hospital department, and he was free. Monday, he would go to a hotel until he could get through to Chaparral. He had told Ophelia, "I can't go on without her," and that was all.

But she said to me, "Jennie, we talked ever since you've been in Chaparral, always about you, but almost never mentioned your name. He wants you to try to forgive Maria Luz. She will want to give you a shower, and it will be something Little Mexico has never seen the like of."

Ophelia talked most of the week. She stayed with me during the days, and Hilda stayed with me during the nights. We had nothing to do but talk and think. Ophelia talked; I listened with a part of my mind, but with most of me I dreamed and planned.

Only permanent guests and a couple who had been stranded in Chaparral were in the Vidaurri. Bert and Lou had some food, but Lee had a grocery store, among which was a gallon of peanut butter. (I used to like peanut butter — before the flood.)

"Jennie must learn to be forgiving. Always, we must forgive or tolerate those who do not want forgiveness. Jennie must learn." Juan had told her.

. . . I could forgive Maria Luz only because my life was going to right itself in spite of her efforts in the past to stop it . . . All of the Mexicans would come to my shower . . . What would we do with an elaborate coffee service? The Anglos who came would be the ones who wanted to come . . . Never would there

159

*be another shower like Ophelia's . . . but never had Anglos gone
to a shower in a Mexican home here . . . I would know who
were my friends; our friends . . .*

"Do you have any idea what a welding of nationalities will
begin to take place if you let Maria give you a shower?"

For one time only — but a beginning. Lee would give us a
Mexican tablecloth, and Hilda would give me some hand embroidered cup towels. The Mexicans would give me what they
call, 'my poor little gift,' and I would be enchanted with the
authentic, painstakingly long, Mexican handwork and pottery.
Lou and Bert would give me a gift. Lou would come to the
shower. Some of the ranch wives would be there — I was not
sure who.

"Juan told Maria, when she and the doctor went to the jail,
that your favorite color is pink. She will probably have a pink
color scheme that will drown us all."

I never said my favorite color was pink. I told Juan I needed
a pink paper flower to go over my ear. I guess it was the pink
dress. Only because I never got the new piece of green gingham
cut out.

"A Mexican shower, given by a person like Maria Luz, is an
elaborate thing, you can't imagine, Jennie. The refreshments
are so many and so varied they make you sick but you have to
taste of everything."

In Mexico City she was one of the most popular hostesses.
What would I wear? I could not afford a dress to go with this
type of entertainment.

"She would, herself and her maids, move all the gifts to
where you would want them after the shower."

*. . . I have no where . . . to Juan's apartment, I guess . . .
Panchito had a loose tooth the last day we had school . . . I
pulled it with a string tied to the door knob . . . Then, they
all had started worrying with a special tooth, to loosen it, and
got in line to say, "Ticher, the tooth, she is to be pulling."*

"Jennie, you're not listening. Don't you want me to tell
you about the shopping?"

. . . the shopping? I could not go shopping until I got paid,

160

and then I could never afford the things to wear to the shower to say nothing of the wedding . . . what did they wear . . . ?

"You won't have to buy a thing to keep house. Juan has everything for housekeeping, and Jennie, the gifts you will get — you will never have to buy another thing. The Mexicans give gifts of money sometimes, but probably not for you, because, though Juan is not wealthy, he does have money from our grandmother."

Finally, I spoke. "Ophelia, you know what I make and where it goes. I won't have the money ever to buy the clothes I will need."

She looked as though she did not know I was serious. "Didn't you know that in a Mexican wedding the man buys everything? I mean absolutely everything that you will wear?"

"Good Lord, no." I said. "In an American wedding . . . "

"You can have an American wedding if you're married in the church here, but even then Juan would want to furnish all the money. Why, he could not face the Mexicans if he didn't."

"I wouldn't get married here. I'd get married in the Mexican Baptist Mission at Holtville. All my Mexicans would come and the Anglos who wanted to. Then, I would know."

"That would be up to you. The wedding day is truly the bride's day to the Mexican."

. . . Ticher, Redbud he have three babies . . . We underestimated you, Redbud . . .

I came out of my reverie enough to say, smilingly, "Ophelia, we're planning Juan's and my future, and Juan may not agree."

"I know what Juan wants for his future, and how he has fought admitting it, even to himself. Why once, Jennie, he told me, 'I hope the man who marries Jennie will let her have pink roses. She should have a carpet of pink roses under her feet and a corsage of pink roses at her waist.'"

"What do you mean, let her have?" I asked.

"Why, a Mexican wedding is all white, even to the stockings. Not a color is on the bride's body, all white for purity, and . . . "

"I know what for, but even stockings?"

. . . I would not mind anything, Juan, if this is the way you want it . . .

161

"And what fun, shopping. A female member of his family goes shopping with you. He gives her the money, and we will shop together. What fun it is, with all that money and you get what you want, except he said once, 'Jennie should have a pink wool coat. Her little spring coat is worn, but she does not know it. I wish it would be all right for me to buy her a pink spring coat.' That's when I decided to give you my pink cashmere sweater — when I could find an excuse."

. . . *Chacha would scatter the pink rose petals on the carpet in front of me as I walked down the aisle. . . I could hear Pedro, in my mind, singing in the background my favorite love song, "Tell Me Why." And it was as real, as if today were the day, but Juan was in jail . . .*

On Wednesday the downpour stopped more suddenly than it had started. We continued to eat the peanut butter. On Friday the highways were open, but only on the pavement. The water was still rolling across the streets, and up on the veranda, but there was no water in the lobby. As far as we could see there still looked to be a solid sheet of water. The water came on in full force, not just a trickle for drinking, and I heated a little and had a sort of bath and put on clean jeans. Debris still floated around and was being constantly pushed off the highway, but a small section was kept cleared on the roads.

Friday afternoon, Cava knocked on my door and said, "Miss Jennie, that Mr. Orgin, he downstairs."

I almost knocked Cava down getting out of my room.

He was standing in the door, clean shaven, recently clean, muddy now, in jeans and plaid shirt. He was smiling as if he had "just come home." His oriental eyes were almost closed.

I took his hand and pulled him out to the corner of the veranda where the water was still above our ankles.

Bert called, "Come back in here. You can talk in the lobby or go up to your room. You'll drown out there. Mr. Ortega, bring her back in."

Ophelia said, "Leave her alone. She knows what she's doing."

We were standing in the water as we put our arms around each other. The pale sunlight was shining on his wet, blue-black hair and the drops of rain on his face were cold.

162

"Jennie," he said, "I don't want to live without you. I tried and I can't. I know now I can't."

I could say nothing at first, but he knew and then I exclaimed, "Juan, look! As far as you can see there is nothing but water. There is no river. It looks like the ocean. Juan, there is no river to cross."

"Yes, my sweet, it looks just a little like the ocean, but not so very much. The ocean is green or blue. Get your sweater. I want to show you the river."

Ophelia handed me the pink sweater. They were all standing in the door as if they were watching a parade.

Lee said, "Can't they see all the water they'll ever want to see from here? They'll drown."

Ophelia said sweetly, "Hush, Lee. They know what they're doing, and I know what he means." She and Juan gave each other a knowing look.

I was in the red Buick, in daylight, riding slowly down the main street in Chaparral with a Mexican — sitting close. I had thought it would take years to get this far. A policeman said, "You're O. K., Mr. Ortega, if you stay on the highway and take it slow. Take it easy." Just as if Juan was anybody. I realized I had not done this. Ophelia and Lee and Bunk and so many people had contributed to today, but mostly Ophelia.

Juan drove slowly, carefully, and quietly out the highway and turned off on the Holt Ranch Road. He stopped the car on a bit of pavement, on the little hill where we could see the wide expanse of water and somewhere down there was the river.

He put his arm around me, and I put my head on his shoulder. He said, "Look at me, Jennie. I want to tell you how it will be. All our lives long you will be the one who will face the crowd even though I spend my life in front of you, fighting for you, all my days. You will have to hear nothing, but be stronger than I am always. You will have to rise above the disapproval of the crowd."

I smiled to myself as he contined for I, too, had memorized Mary Alice Jimenez' letter, but I would not tell him that now. I realized the letter had had much to do with his decision to go away and to try to stay away. My thoughts — dreams — imaginings mixed with the conversation so that I did not always know whether I had thought it, or really said it.

163

. . . Mary Alice Jimenez, you knew . . . somewhere now, beside the Golden River, you know . . . It had to be like this, but it had to be right . . . So, you sent him away . . . You knew that we would each have to know . . .

"She sent me this ring," he said. "It was her wedding ring, and she thought, perhaps, you would keep it or you might like it on a chain."

. . . You knew I would wear it on my wedding finger as long as I lived, didn't you . . . ?

It was a wide silver band which had once been quite intricately engraved but was now worn thin and faded.

"I want it for my wedding ring," I said; and he smiled a deeply content smile.

"No! Don't try it on. It is bad luck. It will fit. Ophelia tried it beside your class ring." Juan put it in his pocket and said, "She sent the little note for you."

> You will never know what might have been,
> Had you taken another road.
> You will always know that you chose then,
> Your pathway, in the long ago.

"This would be true of any decision to marry," I said.

"But this is not any decision, any marriage. It is a decision between the races. Listen, carefully," he said. And, his almost-closed oriental eyes looked into mine. "I want to tell you about the river. Please remember that no decision is final until that decision has been fulfilled."

And he told me: "A long time ago, Ophelia told me about your telling her, and the others, that the river had three sides.

. . . Dearly Beloved, we are gathered together . . .

She understood, only she, then. But, Jennie, I understand. Look at the river. No, don't look at me. Look at the river. It will not be easy living out a whole lifetime with this river. The river will always be the third party. We may be side by side, on this side, that side or in the middle. The middle, what you call the third side. It is dangerous there, Jennie, and there we may bog down.

164

Our hands could break. This is up to us, Jennie, to keep a tight hold on the hands. One of us will at times help the other one out of the middle onto one side of the river. If we do not do this we go down in the quicksand which will forever be all around us, threatening to pull us under. Do you know this, my Jennie?"

. . . to unite this couple in holy matrimony . . .

"You're so serious. I'm not sure you want to marry me," I said.

"I was never so sure in my life," he replied. "But you, too, must be sure. Do you have any idea how long is, 'till death do us part'?"

. . . In sickness and in health; in poverty and in wealth . . .

I said, "Look at it Juan. You told me once that when it was solid sand — now, it is solid water. There is no river. No river to cross."

"I, too, would like to think that, but that is not the way it will be. It could stay under water or be solid sand, always, but for generations yet it will be there influencing our future and the lives of future generations."

. . . not too white; not too dark . . .

He said, "Jennie, do you realize that all of your descendants will be Mexicans? All of them. If the name of Ortega lasts a thousand years, or four thousand, or perhaps the name may die out, but not the part that is Ortega — always your descendants will be Mexicans."

. . . Jennie, do you take this man . . .

"I understand that all of my descendants will be some part Mexican. I will consider them and their problems if I am here, as Mary Alice considered us." I said this after thinking I would not mention her name.

. . . Juan, do you take this woman . . .

He smiled the age-old Latin smile of the generations passed and said, "She knew, Jennie. She left a note to have the ring sent after her death. She knew how it would be. Once, she too, looked across this river and pondered."

165

. . . to be your lawful wedded husband . . . I do . . .

"*Ah, Jenita mia. Vida de mi alma . . .,*" and I knew he would always go into Spanish in times of stress or great emotion. "I do not wish for you to be a Mexican girl. There is not one thing I would change about you. Always remember that you are an Anglo and be proud. I am a Mexican, and I am proud. Let us be proud and teach our children pride of both races."

. . . to be your lawful wedded wife . . . I do . . .

"Never lose identity with your race," he continued. "Let me be a Mexican, as I shall try to let you be an Anglo. I do not want to take away from you; I want to add to you. Keep all of yourself that you can. You will lose enough of yourself by being married to me."

. . . My Dearly Loved Husband . . .

Then he said, "Races are so different in so many ways. I — the Mexican am a jealous, possessive man."

"Juan Ortega, I am a jealous woman and never forget it!"
He smiled, the slow, happy smile which was his own.
He said, "Try to understand, so that you will have not so much hurt when things do not go right. Now, we will go back to the hotel. I want to give Ophelia the money to take you shopping for your wedding things. We will get married where and in the way you like. We will go down to the little place in Chihuahua I told you about. I think you will be happier there because . . ."
"We will get married in Holtville in the Mexican Baptist Mission and go to Little Mexico. There we will stay."
"Whatever you want," he said, trying not to show too much happiness.
"Stop the car! Wait! Listen!" I said.
Across the long valley, on the Mexican side, clear and sweet, I could hear the church bells resounding across the water, and I knew that this was my future — our future. Somewhere down there, in the inundated valley, was the river; there would always be the river. Your side — my side; your people — my people; our side — our people. I saw the unpredictable future. I would